COOL

MARY W. WALTERS

River Books
an imprint of The Books Collective

See page 211 for the publication history of each story.

Published by River Books
an imprint of The Books Collective
214-21 10405 Jasper Avenue
Edmonton, Alberta, Canada T5J 3S2

River Books and The Books Collective acknowledge the support of the Canada Council for the Arts and the City of Edmonton / Edmonton Arts Council for our publishing programme.

The author gratefully acknowledges support for her writing in general from the Alberta Foundation for the Arts, and support for this short story collection in particular from the Canada Council and the former Literary Arts Branch of the former Alberta Culture. Many thanks also to Timothy J. Anderson, my editor, who helped me to bring this home.

Editor for the press: Candas Jane Dorsey. Outside editor: Timothy J. Anderson. Cover design: Duncan Campbell. Cover image: Duncan Campbell. Interior typeset in Minion and Sanvito on 50lb offset. Cover printed on 10pt Cornwall cover stock.

Canadian Cataloguing in Publication Data
Walters, Mary W.
Cool

ISBN 1-895836-72-7

I. Title
PS8595.A599C66 2000 C813'.54 C00-910640-5
PR9199.3.W344C66 2000

1 2 3 4 5 04 03 02 01 00

PRINTED AND BOUND IN CANADA BY PRIORITY PRINTING LTD, EDMONTON.

To my significant elders—
Marney, Barbara, Sammy, Tedi and Claire—
with love.

Table of Contents

Last Respects

This house is not so silent as it seemed when I sat down here on the chesterfield a little while ago. Aunt Isabel is resting in her room at the end of the hall, but I can hear the squeak of the springs in her bed and from time to time a sort of strangled sigh, the last muffled remnants of her weeping. The small white refrigerator in the kitchen stutters into silence for just long enough that I forget it, then gurgles back to life again. I have never been so irritated by such tiny sounds.

My book lies open in my lap. My eyes move across the lines until some bit of punctuation stops me and I realize that I haven't understood a single word. Last night, it wasn't until Aunt Isabel had called three times for me to turn out my light that I at last unwillingly slid the marker between these pages and, cursing her silently, set it on the small blue table by my bed. How I want to be drawn back into the power of these words, but I can't. The details of this house, this room refuse to let me be.

Aunt Isabel's broadloom is the colour of uncut grass and the velvet of her chairs and chesterfield is almost the same deep green. The other furniture is all very old, and the wood seems to glow somewhere just beneath the surface. No dust would dare to settle on these pieces, and the laundry is never spilled out on the couch to be sorted as it is at home.

The house is too big for one person. Aunt Isabel says so herself.

When Uncle William was still alive, she'd say, "You know, this house is really too big for two." She was right then, too, but I don't imagine she'll ever move now. The house reminds her of William, she says. Funny. You'd think she'd want to move away from all of that, to forget.

The doorbell rings and as I stand my book slides onto the carpet with a thump.

"Would you get that, Emmie?" calls Aunt Isabel. She's making little grunts as she bends to squeeze her swollen feet into her tiny shoes. Aunt Isabel would never receive visitors in her bedroom slippers, as my mother sometimes does.

I retrieve my book and start toward the hallway. Aunt Isabel is right behind me as I pull open the big oak door and unlock the screen.

It's Dr. Watson, his white hair shining under the light, one thin hand waving away the moths that are batting themselves against the bulb. He ducks his head a little as he comes through the doorway, a gesture I've often wondered at because although he's a tall man, the top of his head is several inches from the door frame. Maybe he used to be taller.

He is immaculately dressed, as usual, in a deep grey pinstripe suit, a maroon tie with tiny white dots knotted carefully over a starched white shirt. A thin gold tie-clip is his only jewellery.

My mother told me once when I asked her that he was almost sixty and that no, he'd never married, although she wasn't sure what business that was of mine.

"George," says Aunt Isabel. "How kind of you to come." She smiles the grim little smile she was wearing for me when she returned from the hospital at noon.

"She was a fine woman, Isabel," he says, and then he catches both my hands in his before I can move away. His blue eyes are moist behind his thick glasses. Please, God, don't let him cry.

"I am so sorry, Emmie," he says.

I nod, and hope my smile is less tight than my aunt's. I don't like it here, standing between them. I can smell her heavy, expensive perfume, and the air in this small wood-panelled vestibule is growing sickly sweet and hot.

"Would you like some tea?" I ask.

"Perhaps a brandy for the doctor, Em," Aunt Isabel says. "And pour a tiny sherry for me."

The kitchen, where Aunt Isabel keeps her small supply of liquor in a lower cupboard, is a brighter and less cluttered room than the others in her house. The walls and ceiling have recently been painted white and the pale green floor and marbled counter tops gleam under the coil of fluorescent light. I close the swinging door behind me and walk over to the window. I press my nose against the screen, wanting to inhale some of the cool darkness of the August night, but I can smell only the dust and metal of the screen itself. Somewhere out there in that night is Scott, perhaps already dressed and standing at his window, waiting until it's time to come for me. I rub my hand across my nose in case the screen has left a mark, and turn to get the drinks.

There is a heavy rosewood cabinet with five glass doors against one wall. Anyone else would have put a table there, but Aunt Isabel always eats in the dining room, always uses silver and china and linen table napkins, even when she is alone.

When I was smaller and my mother brought me here to visit, I would sit on the high white stool near the sink and listen to my mother and her sister talk as they peeled carrots and potatoes, sliced onions, shelled peas. My mother began to cry one day when Aunt Isabel mentioned my father's name. Mother said it was the onions that made her weep and I couldn't see how they could be sad about someone who'd been dead for as long as I could remember, but even then I was uncomfortable with adult tears no matter what their provocation. And I looked away from them, at the rows and rows of polished glass and crystal in the rosewood cabinet. There were little glass animals in there too, blown glass my mother told me, very fragile. I wished that I could take out some of the shining pieces myself to look at them more closely, but I knew better than to ask.

Now, for the first time, I am permitted, unsupervised, to open the glass doors. The tiny swans and the giraffe are no longer of interest to me, and I take out a short, full-bellied glass for the brandy, and a taller one with a stem for Aunt Isabel.

She's probably crying again. I wonder whether she's being held by Dr. Watson. I try to imagine that, him so tall and thin with his long awkward arms around her short plump body, her thick grey hair against the charcoal of his suit. I can't imagine it, and I don't want to see it. Slowly, very slowly, I carry the glasses to the counter, walking on tiptoe so they won't remember that I'm here.

I'm glad Dr. Watson didn't try to hug me. Aunt Isabel did, when she told me, and I wanted to break away and run from her warm thickness, her misery, which I can't lessen or share.

There used to be more bottles in this cupboard when Uncle William was alive. I read the label on each one as I take it out and place it on the counter beside the glasses. The brandy bottle is tall and made of smoked green glass, and another says, "Harvey's Bristol Cream." Sherry. I wonder if its taste is as warm and smooth as its name. The other bottles I place back on the shelf, making a game of it, trying not to make a sound.

I do not know the taste of brandy or sherry. My mother doesn't approve of children "taking spirits." I do, however, know the taste of rye whiskey and gin, and I'm not fond of either of them. In an hour, Scott and Ted and the others will bring their bottles of Coke and Orange Crush, already mixed with liquor, to Wanda's party. They will have replaced the metal bottle caps carefully, so Mr. and Mrs. Collier will not suspect. And I will have a drink then, enough that

Scott can smell it on my breath, and after that I will tip back the pop bottle against my lips when they pass it to me, and pretend. Perhaps if they brought Harvey's Bristol Cream, I would do better.

There will be music, too, at Wanda's party and we will dance, fast dances at the beginning, then slow ones later on, when Wanda thinks her parents are asleep. Someone, Ted perhaps, will turn off the light and under the camouflage of the Ventures, there will be whispering and some rustling of clothes and Wanda will squeal, "No, Ted!" more to let us know he's trying something than to stop him. Scott's mouth will be pressed close and hard against mine, and the air will be electric with excitement edged with the fear that Wanda's parents might not really be asleep at all.

Scott will be here, at the front door, in less than an hour.

The front door squeaks open and I stop what I'm doing to listen. It's Mrs. McNeill, my aunt's chattering little neighbour. Isabel's greeting sounds controlled enough, and I carry the two glasses through the darkened dining room and into the living room.

"Oh, Emmie, you poor dear," cries Mrs. MacNeill. My aunt and Dr. Watson are standing at the far end of the room and the birdlike neighbour is hurrying across the room, her arms open, and I hold the glasses in front of me so that she can't come closer without spilling them.

"Your mother was such a wonderful woman. But this is best for her. You understand that, don't you?" Her voice is hoarse and tragic, her hands now clasped together in front of her. "Her pain is over."

"Can I get you some sherry?" I ask.

She shakes her head slowly, her eyes wide with disbelief, then turns to Isabel, who shrugs.

I hand the brandy to the doctor and the sherry to my aunt. Suddenly it seems very dark and small in here, and I look for a light to turn on. But all the lamps are glowing brightly.

Mrs. MacNeill sits on the opposite end of the dark green couch from Dr. Watson. Her hands pull at a Kleenex in her lap, and she looks at the doctor intently as she speaks.

"I'm so glad you're here, Doctor. For the sake of poor Isabel. And dear Emmie, of course. I was afraid they might have been alone. People shouldn't be alone at a time like this. Companionship. That's the best medicine for grief, I always say."

She looks over at my aunt, who nods.

"I would have been here earlier myself," Mrs. MacNeill continues, "but I just couldn't leave my Ben. His ulcer's really acting up these days. His doctor says bicarbonate of soda, but it doesn't seem to help a bit. I guess you know all about ulcers, don't you, Doctor? They're very hard to manage."

On and on she prattles, and Dr. Watson's face is turned toward her, but I can tell from his eyes that he's not listening.

He has twisted his feet around one another until his legs are wrapped from the knees down, exposing white, hairless flesh above his grey socks. Dr. Watson is the only person I've ever met who could do that, and it fascinates me. When he came to visit us at home, when my mother was still able to sit up in the living room for a while, I would watch him wrap and unwrap his legs, wishing I were out instead with Scott. And then, after I'd done the dishes and turned out the hall light, I'd sit on the edge of my bed and try to twist my feet like that. I couldn't do it. Even if I'd been able to, I couldn't have shown anyone. Mother dislikes me making fun of adults.

I haven't seen Dr. Watson in several weeks. He visited every Wednesday and Sunday evening when my mother was still at home. He used to walk right into her bedroom and take her pulse and blood pressure, and then he'd help her into the living room where they had tea and the store-bought coffee cake my mother sent me out for. They talked, about the government and the Bay of Pigs and other things I didn't know or care about. The way Dr. Watson looked at my mother with such pity and tenderness usually drove me to my homework. Later, he helped her back to bed, and she was very slow and thin as she leaned against his arm.

It was Dr. Watson who called the ambulance the day she could no longer stand even with assistance, and Dr. Watson who drove me to Aunt Isabel's and told me in the car that my mother had inoperable cancer. He told me very gently what that meant. I didn't believe him.

Aunt Isabel sits in Uncle William's armchair, her head against the antimacassar on the headrest, her hand tight around the lace-edged handkerchief in her lap. I doubt she's ever used a Kleenex.

I would like to go back to the kitchen or to my room, but I must tell them I'm going out, somehow, when the right moment comes along. And so I sit on the needlepoint footstool near the dining room, as far from their pale and thinly disguised sadness as I can get. Aunt Isabel's curtains, I notice, have a thick layer of dust across the top of them. Perhaps she can't reach that high, to dust them or to get them down. Perhaps she hasn't noticed. It surprises me; it's so unlike her.

"I suppose it's too early to think of arrangements," says Mrs. MacNeill. Dr. Watson sits up suddenly and looks around him the way my grandmother used to do when the sermon was over.

"Geoff can't be here until Thursday," says Aunt Isabel.

My mother's brother lives in Vancouver and has never in his life done anything in a hurry.

"So will it be Thursday or Friday, do you think?" Mrs. MacNeill, I'm certain, won't let up until she has an answer.

"I really don't know yet. Friday, I guess. I'll have to call Forrester's in the morning." Aunt Isabel looks as though she may begin to weep again. I stand up to turn on a light, and then remember that they are all on. They look at me. I look at my watch and sit down again. Fifteen minutes.

Mrs. MacNeill clears her throat. "Well, now, Isabel. I don't want you to worry about anything. I'll start on the sandwiches and things for after the … for Friday. I can handle the whole thing." She begins a list of fillings she'll prepare for the sandwiches – egg and tuna and roast beef – but Aunt Isabel interrupts to offer a cup of tea. Aunt Isabel sounds tired, but Mrs. MacNeill accepts immediately, and leans back in the corner of the couch.

And then she asks my aunt what it was like, "For Edith, at the end."

I can't believe her question, don't even understand it for a moment. But Aunt Isabel doesn't take offence, seems almost relieved to have been asked. Before she can say a word, I jump to my feet.

"Scott's coming for me in a little while. I'm going out. I'll make the tea."

"Tonight?" Aunt Isabel asks. "You're going out tonight?"

I don't answer. I run into the kitchen, wishing the door would slam instead of swinging so slowly back and forth.

I can breathe more easily here, don't feel so trapped and suffocated. I touch the school ring on my left hand for reassurance, touch the heavy roll of adhesive tape on the inside. At last the tape is grey and dirty. Some girls, like Wanda, can't hang onto a ring for long enough for that to happen. But Scott and I are different. He's older than the others in our class, and this ring means more to us than it would to Wanda or Ted.

When I'm with him, I'm free of all of this. When we're together, there's just his hand around mine, the clean smell of his shirt against my face. With him, there's a promise for the future that none of these adults can take away or spoil.

The kitchen door squeaks open and Dr. Watson comes in. I take down the teapot and rinse it with boiling water, not looking at him.

"Emmie?"

"Yes, Sir?"

"I've known your family a long time. Longer than you can remember, I've no doubt. I know you feel very alone right now, and I want to tell you that I share your grief. I loved your mother very much."

Oh, God, no. Don't tell me this. I don't want to hear it, and I don't want to see you cry.

I hear the crunch of tires on the gravel outside and I turn in relief from Dr. Watson.

"See you later," I call, as I run past the living room and out of the front door.

The air is cool against my face and I inhale it deeply. It smells so good out here – like freshly cut grass – as though the night air had been scented for my pleasure. The breeze stirs the oak trees at the edge of the park and I look up at them and up again, and the sky has never seemed so vast, so alive with winking points of light.

The Perfect Parent

Polly Prewitt was a perfect parent, or as close to one as any human being can reasonably expect to get considering the materials parents have to work with. She'd suspected this for many years, although she was careful not to speak of it to anyone, including her husband, for she was also sensitive to other people's feelings. But it gave her a certain satisfaction to know that her children would be far-better-adjusted adults for having been raised by as conscientious a parent as she.

When friends discussed their children's bed-wetting problems, she gave little clicks of sympathy and quietly savoured the fact that her boys had both been trained before their second birthdays, and without a single tear or relapse. When other people mentioned the abysmal eating habits of their offspring, Polly gently let it be known that her boys ate what she gave them or did not eat at all. She made no fuss about it with them, she said, and they ate: spinach, tofu, the whole works.

Polly nurtured her pride by reading covers of magazines in stores. "Are you passing on gender stereotypes to your children?" Nope, she mentally responded. Her husband William did the dishes every other night and made dinner for them all on Sundays. Polly had taken a course in automotive mechanics specifically so the boys would never get the idea that Mothers Cooked and Fathers Fixed Cars. And she had not said a single word against it when Ricky demanded a doll last summer. She wrote it down on her list and bought it for him at Christmas; that way he learned he did not get everything he wanted at the moment he asked for it. It was a cuddly doll, a male baby doll, anatomically correct. The fact that by Christmastime Ricky was in kindergarten and refused to play with it – the other little boys had told him that dolls were for girls – was beside the point.

Jamie had learned that One Takes Responsibility for One's Actions when he kicked the front wheel of his bicycle off centre in a fit of temper and could not ride it until he'd saved enough from his allowance to pay for the repair.

Her boys were in good shape, she thought cheerfully. And so was she.

And then one day she was standing in the checkout line at Safeway, frowning to herself at the boxes of sugar-coated cereal in the cart of the woman ahead of her, when a brightly coloured magazine caught her eye. She looked up. There, in bold red letters on the cover, was a question that stopped her cold.

"Has your child learned to deal with loss?" it said.

Loss? Loss? She'd never even thought of that, and here was Jamie almost nine and Ricky already past his sixth birthday. She snatched a copy of the magazine and tossed it, front cover down, into her cart.

She read the article covertly before the boys came home from school. She read it twice. The writer urged her to allow her children grief in little ways, so they would be better able later to handle major loss. A pet, the author said, is a perfect medium for teaching such a lesson.

"Do not ever attempt to replace a pet until the grief has been worked through," the article advised. It went on to point out the identifiable stages of grief: denial, anger, finally acceptance.

Polly's boys had missed all that, and she would certainly need to set the matter right. What if something terrible happened to her or William or, God forbid, to any of their school friends, and she had not prepared them for it?

All right. A pet, she thought, as she watched Ricky and Jamie brush their teeth that night, before she read them their story. Jamie preferred to read to himself, but she insisted. She knew that reading aloud fostered closeness between parent and child.

A dog would be too much trouble, she decided, and by the time it was ready to teach its lesson in grief, the boys would probably be living elsewhere, attending university or sweeping streets. (Whatever life course they chose was fine with her.) A dog, or a cat, would simply take too long.

Polly couldn't stand rodents, so mice were out, and birds could live for years.

"Fish!" she said, firmly closing the book in the middle of a chapter.

"What?" said Ricky.

"Nothing," said Polly, opening the book again.

Next day, when their father had taken them to swimming lessons, she went to Sears and bought a big glass fishbowl and a guppy that looked suspiciously pregnant. She bought fish food and received instructions in the care and feeding of fish. She did not admit to the salesclerk that her intention was for the fish to die. In fact, she knew she wouldn't be able to help sustaining its little life for as long as possible. Polly was an honourable woman.

The boys were delighted with her offering. The bowl was given a position of prominence, on the coffee table in the living room. Ricky and Jamie watched the little brown being swim around for hours on end. Ricky asked at one point if he could take it out and play with it, but Jamie told him that fishes can't live outside the water. Ricky didn't want the fish to die, did he? Ricky solemnly said, "No."

Polly looked on, approving.

She did not tell William of her plan because he'd only ask her at breakfast how her 'ghoulish death experiment' was coming along, or words to that effect. He was capable of ruining everything when he didn't understand her motives, and she had suspicions he would not understand them this time. There are things a parent has to do alone.

Polly changed the water regularly and fed her little charge, and it thrived. After a week or so, the boys lost interest in it, and so she gave it a name to foster their feelings of warmth and attachment toward it. "Jean," she called it, a suitably androgynous name. The guppy had not yet produced any little guppies (which would have been a bonus: two lessons for the price of one), and William said all fish were rounder in the middle than they were towards the ends. She let the boys feed it, but even that bored them rather quickly, and they told her that since she'd bought it, she could feed it. Responsibility for one's actions coming back at her.

~

Polly had almost decided that Jean would become a permanent part of the household, and a permanent addition to her daily routine, when she went downstairs and found him/her belly up.

Polly sighed and, her expression appropriately mournful, went up to tell the boys.

"I have some bad news for you," she said when she went into their room. "Our little Jean is dead." ("Tell them the truth!" the article admonished. "Do not tell them the creature has gone to sleep or gone to heaven. Be honest!")

"No kidding," said Ricky, and he began to hum the Oscar Mayer song as he pulled his pyjamas off.

"Can I see it?" Jamie asked.

That was better. "Let them see the body of the pet," the article went on. "Let them confront their grief, hug the pet and cry." Hugging was out, but the principle remained.

"Of course. You both can." She led them down to the living room and stood back to observe their reactions.

"Hm," said Jamie. "What'll we do with it?"

"We can bury it out in the garden, if you like. Together. The three of us."

"Great!" Ricky said, and he ran off, half-clad, to get his shovel from the sandbox.

"Naw. I'll be late for school and I promised I'd bring the soccer ball. Let's just flush it."

So Ricky and Polly buried the little bit of fish, and Jamie left for school. (Denial, Polly thought. He's not confronting this issue. It takes time to come to terms with loss.) Ricky seemed more interested in a worm his shovel had unearthed than in the farewell to Jean, but Polly was satisfied. At least he had been present.

She waited for the boys' reactions, but they never once mentioned the death of the fish. At last she took the fishbowl, clean and polished and very empty-looking, and she put it on the kitchen table to emphasize their loss. It was cruel, but it had to be done.

"Can I have it for an ant house?" Jamie asked.

"No! I want to collect bugs to keep in it," Ricky said. "How come he always gets everything?"

Ants. Polly turned the possibility over in her mind. At least Jamie would have a commitment to his ants. He'd wanted them, and the loss would be greater for his having been the instigator. Ants it would be.

"Well, Ricky," she said. "Jamie spoke first this time, and I've told you often enough before that life's not necessarily fair." She looked at Jamie. "Go ahead and start your ant colony, but I'm going to carry this out on the sun deck. I won't have them in the house."

It took less than a week for all the ants to escape, and they did not seem to have set up any domestic arrangements in the bowl at all during their brief stay. Polly found Jamie on the sun deck after school one day, staring glumly at the pile of dirt he had poured from the fishbowl onto the indoor/outdoor carpet. She did not mention the mess. He had enough to deal with, poor little tyke, having to confront all this so early on in life. But it was good, she thought, as she saw a tear roll down his cheek.

She went out and sat beside him. "Do you want to talk about it?" she asked.

"I feel sick," he said.

"That's the sadness, dear. Nothing lasts forever, you know. All things must go away or die at some time or another."

"No, Mom. That's not it. My stomach hurts," Jamie said, and then he threw up on the lifeless anthill.

It turned out to be chicken pox, and he was home for a week.

~

"Now, bugs!" Ricky clapped his hands when he saw the fishbowl sitting clean and once more empty on the kitchen table.

"All right. But this is your last chance."

"Last chance for what?" asked William, looking up from a forkful of shepherd's pie.

"Oh, nothing. I'm just tired of pets, that's all."

Ricky collected a ladybug and two little green things and a fly before he, too, was stricken with chicken pox. He'd covered the top of the jar with a piece of plastic wrap with holes poked in it and thrown in a leaf or two for food. He'd given each bug a name and spent a long time watching his captives in the bowl. He'd left them on the sun deck when he began to feel unwell.

One morning, spotted but recovering, he recalled his menagerie and went downstairs to find them dead.

"Humph," he said and went back to bed, leaving Polly to rinse the bowl once more.

In the afternoon, she found a piece of paper on which Ricky had written his name backward. Reversed writing was, she knew, a sign of deeper problems. Ricky was reacting. She leaned the paper against the empty fish/ant/bug bowl.

"Tell me why you did this," she asked him gently when he came down to supper.

"Did what?"

"Wrote your name backwards. Did you notice you had done it?"

Ricky shrugged. "Jamie bet me a nickel that I couldn't."

"That's it! I've had it!" Polly, the almost-perfect parent shouted. She ran downstairs and wrote a caustic note to the perpetrator of the nonsense in the magazine.

"Loss," she noted in conclusion, "is not a big problem for well adjusted kids. If everything else is going smoothly, they do not react to it at all."

She felt better then, almost restored, and she went back to the dinner table.

"You've been awfully tense lately," William said as she carried her plate to the sink and submerged it in the soapy water.

"I just got a little carried away with something," she said. "It was no big deal. As I'd suspected, everything around here is just fine. And I," she said, lifting the empty glass bowl into the air, "am turning this into a terrarium."

"What's a..." Jamie said, as the bowl slipped from her hands and smashed to smithereens on the kitchen floor.

There was a stunned silence as the four of them studied the remains of the bowl.

Then, tumult.

"What d'ja do that for?" Jamie shouted. "I wanted that bowl to keep my rock collection in."

Ricky started to cry. "I wanted to get a turtle."

Polly stared at them in astonishment. "Keep your voices down, you crazy kids," she said. "It's just a bowl. I can get another one tomorrow."

She stopped and watched their shuddering shoulders and listened to their sobs.

Then she said quietly, "No, I guess I can't," and went to get the broom.

Afternoon Visit

"Mom. Come with me. Please."

Rachel made her voice more insistent this time.

The women stopped talking and the sun porch steamed in the silence. This time, her mother did not flick a glance at her and then look away again. Instead she paused and glanced at the others and prepared herself to speak, shifting slightly in her chair. Before she said a word, Rachel knew there'd been no point in trying.

"With all of the independence you show most of the time," her mother said, "I really am surprised." She was using those words because of the other women, Rachel thought. She spoke differently when she was alone with Rachel, and yet another way when Harold was around.

"Last year you were only twelve, and you didn't have a problem then, did you? No bears? No snakes?" Rachel's mother smiled at the other women, shaking her head in mild exasperation.

Rachel sat down again in the wicker chair by the door, and smoothed the apple-green fabric of her little-girl dress over her knees. All of them, the three aunts she barely knew and her mother, were looking at her.

"Well?"

"I guess so. I won't go, after all."

Her mother lowered her fine eyebrows almost imperceptibly, a warning, and placed her teacup on the table beside her elbow as she turned back to her conversation. Her stockings made a slight slicking noise as she crossed her legs at the ankles, and the sound added to Rachel's discomfort.

Her mother was trying to tell the other women everything she and Rachel had done since they last got together without once mentioning Harold. This effort had caused her not to speak less, as one might have thought, but to become more talkative than usual – as though by eliminating silences she could prevent the other women's thoughts from wandering into the areas she'd cordoned off. The others passed around and back events from their own lives like plates of cookies, and their voices rose and fell through the heat of the afternoon.

Rachel did not mind that her mother had not chosen to speak of Harold here. If her mother never mentioned Harold again, it would be fine with her. He was a cripple and an idiot, and the way her mother fawned on him was sickening. When Rachel absolutely had to go somewhere with them, she was horrified that they might run into someone that she knew – someone who would see Harold and her mother holding hands and acting stupid, and then would see who the girl was with them. She stayed as far away from them as she could when they were out in public.

From across the clearing, through the screen which Rachel's head was almost touching, through the line of scalp that separated her braids, came the steady, chunk, chunk of the axe against the wood, each shock of sound a new nudge against her bladder.

She watched Aunt Meg, wondering why this woman with her soft red-grey hair did not pay any attention to the terrible sounds that were coming from the yard. Aunt Meg was Rachel's father's sister, much older than Rachel's mother. She looked like the kind and thoughtful man her mother liked so much to talk about – or had until Harold came along. A woman with a gentle face like that should understand Rachel's problem. She should walk to the screen door and call to her husband, "Miles! You come in out of that heat and have a glass of lemonade. That wood can wait until it's cooler."

Instead, Aunt Meg was telling Rachel's mother how hard it had been to nurse Miles through bronchitis all last winter.

She felt him behind her, waiting between her and the outhouse, and she pressed her legs together. The women would soon move into the kitchen and start to prepare the supper – cold meats and salads, and the sweet brown rolls that Rachel's mother had made the day before and brought with them in the car. When the supper was ready to be served and the table set, all of them would go into the lake to swim.

Rachel knew she couldn't wait that long.

Chunk. Chunk. Chunk: the bite of the axe and then the silence, even more ominous, as he stopped to wipe his forehead with a sweat-soaked handkerchief, or maybe to light a cigarette. Keeping her knees and thighs pressed hard together, she gripped the front of the wicker chair, one hand beside each leg. That only made it worse.

Chunk. Chunk. Chunk. Measuring his blows so he'd be able to outlast her.

Last year she'd gone out willingly, bored with the women's chatter in the sun porch and anxious to be outside. She'd gone down to the lake where it was cooler and he'd followed, casually offering to show her the place where the pine tree had been toppled by lightening into the lake. Out of sight of the cottage, he'd caught her by the shoulders, huge arms holding her astonished as he bent and kissed her mouth. Almost as it happened, it was a memory – of hard teeth, rank tobacco-breath, a stained grin as he withdrew – and arms so immense that escaping them had never crossed her mind.

He'd seemed to vanish the moment he released her. "Gone to town for supplies," Aunt Meg had smiled hours later. "Not much for women's visiting, is Miles."

Afterward in the car on the way home, Rachel had said, "I don't want to go back there."

Her mother answered quickly, her eyes on the road. "You're being selfish, Rachel. It's only once a year. It's about the only contact we have with your father's relatives, and I owe it to them. To him." Her voice had taken on the mixture of self-pity and self-righteousness that it always did when she mentioned him.

"It isn't that," she said. "It's Uncle Miles."

"What about Uncle Miles?"

Suddenly Rachel knew that her mother would be angry if she told her what had happened. Why had Rachel gone down to the lake alone? she'd want to know. Why had she followed Miles out of sight of the cottage? What had Rachel expected? She'd let him think it was all right to kiss her. What did she expect if she was going to act like that?

"I don't like the way he looks," she said quietly at last.

Her mother had told her she'd need to be careful when she got older. Boys couldn't always control themselves when there were girls around, she'd said. It was up to her, up to Rachel, to protect herself from them. It was all part of the growing up – the 'developing,' as her mother liked to call it. Rachel should have stayed in the cottage with the women. She could see that now.

Her mother was looking at her. "That's the only reason?"

Rachel nodded, feeling her face flush. It was a little kiss. A little thing. A nothing. If she didn't mention it, it would be like it never happened. Maybe he'd been meaning to be kind. He and Meg had no children of their own, her mother had told her sadly. Maybe he thought children should be kissed.

"He has yellow teeth."

"Just stay away from him, then, if you don't like the way he looks. He's hardly ever around anyway. It's one day at the lake, Rachel. One day every year."

'I don't ask much of you,' her tone said. 'I never ask enough.'

During the winter, unseen herself, she'd seen Harold take her mother in his arms – he had huge arms, too, like Miles, and was proud of how strong they were: as though that could make up for the gimpy, ill-formed leg. He'd pressed his mouth against her mother's mouth, and her mother had leaned into him, eager, hungry to be kissed by him. Seeing them, the memory of Miles had risen in her throat, and she had turned away.

Now she shook her head at Aunt Delia's offer of biscuits and wished that she'd refused all earlier offers of lemonade and cheese and especially the devilled eggs which she felt pressed sour deep inside her. Her body was her enemy, forcing her away from the safety of this female circle. She could not wait another minute.

She stood. "Mother!" she said.

"What?" her mother answered sharply before looking, embarrassed, at the others. "I suppose she's bored with us," she said. To Rachel she added more gently, "You go ahead. Afterwards, you can walk down by the lake."

"Just don't go in without someone to supervise," Aunt Meg said.

She stood at the screen door, her eyes on the path to the outhouse. He was behind the woodshed, out of sight. She heard his steady chopping.

"I don't know how he can stand to do that in this heat," Rachel's mother said.

Rachel paused, hopeful, but Aunt Meg just laughed. "He'll do anything to avoid sitting in here and drinking lemonade with us. Miles is a man's man, I'm afraid." Meg loved her husband with her voice, the same way Rachel's mother's voice stroked Harold when she talked about him.

Rachel didn't like the way her stomach felt. She pushed herself away from them, out the screen door – remembering she was supposed to close it quietly only as it slammed behind her. She ran as quickly as she could down the path, turning her ankles on half-buried roots.

In a moment she was safe inside the outhouse, its door shut, her foot out against it, her knee locked to hold it closed. She held her breath against the smell, face burning from fear and heat.

The silence was broken only by the buzzing of the flies. The chopping sound had stopped when the screen door slammed. Maybe he'd seen that as a signal. A sign from her to him. Maybe nothing would have happened if she hadn't slammed that door. But something would happen now: of that she was certain.

She put the metal hook into its circlet to lock the door and stood, listening for the sound of his thick yellow breath, but there was nothing. She leaned her head against the door. Her bladder empty, she could feel the pounding of her heart against her stomach, the egg wedged bitter, caught. If she wanted to stay here until her mother came to find her, she'd have to do it sitting down with her head between her knees.

A large brown spider weaved slowly through the heat and smell, ready to unfurl a thread between the corrugated roof and her bare neck. Her mother might not come for hours.

She unlatched the door and put her head out. The cooler, cleaner air in her nostrils made her feel a little better. She put one foot out, then the other, not breathing, and marked the pathway with her eyes that would lead her back to the safety of the sun porch. Perhaps she could outrun him.

His hand closed around her arm. As he drew her out through the thick camouflage of trees to the place where he'd been working, she heard herself make a low, thick sound. She'd thought that she was screaming.

"There you are, my bad little girl," he said, deep and almost whispering. "You almost forgot to come give your Uncle Miles his kiss."

She shook her head, trying to pull away, eyes wildly scanning the wood house which hid them from the cottage. His hand was firm, his other arm came around to pull her to him, and as she struggled his warm fleshy lips came down and jammed her head still.

He held her by the waist and easily lifted her onto his bench, grinning sour breath when his head was even with hers.

"Let me look at you," he said. "You're a pretty little girl."

Didn't the women hear that his axe had stopped? Didn't they wonder where she was? He was too close; she was too scared to call.

"I bet the boys like kissing you at school. Don't they? And I bet you let them, don't you?"

She wriggled, but he held her tightly at the waist. Her heart pounded, pounded and there was something in the back of her throat that … something coming loose.

"And I bet you like it, too." She felt his hand come up between her knees and she flinched in horror. The sour egg inside her moved. As his puffy stinking face came closer, her stomach churned and her throat opened and she leaned forward, retching, retching, retching.

With a gasp he let her go and leapt away from her. Still retching, she jumped from the bench and hit the ground in a run, but he was between her and the cottage and she ran into the woods, along the path that took her high above the lake.

She slowed when she could run no further and then she stopped, her breath coming in irregular, painful gasps. The cottage was around the edge of the water, visible from the height she'd reached and close enough to swim to if she dared. But he would see her in the water and he would be waiting for her when she reached the shore. He would kill her with his axe, for doing that to him.

She would wait here, beside this rock, for just one minute until she got her breath, and then she'd run again. If she went further around the bay, she could wait hidden in the trees until the women came out of the cabin. Then she could call to them. Once their eyes were on her, then she would be safe.

Her head ached and pounded in the sunlight and her whole body trembled. Her stupid new dress was wet and smelling of her sickness. Her mother would be angry about that. Never did she mention her widowhood with such reverence as when she thought that money had been wasted.

Did Harold do that to her mother? Put his hand between her legs? Did her mother like that, too? Rachel put her hand against her mouth but there was nothing left in her stomach, and her throat was still.

Then she heard him, moving in the bushes below her. If she ran and he looked up, he'd see her. Numb with renewed fear, she moved silently back behind the rock and crouched.

Nothing happened. She peered out and saw that he was far enough below her that she was not in danger. He was moving around the water's edge toward the cove. He kept looking out across the water toward the cottage – not up, to see where she might be – as he moved through the reeds and grasses by the lake.

Still cautiously, but with her breath now growing even, she raised herself higher so she could see over the edge of the rock. He was directly below her, moving steadily toward her left.

He stopped and, kicking his shoes into the grass, he quickly took off his plaid shirt and threw it into the lake, and then he did the same with his khaki trousers. Without pausing to remove his underpants and socks, he went into the water, too, sinking below the surface. He rose again, rubbing his hair and face and his big rubbery shoulders and pale chest – frantic, she realized, to rid himself of her. Now he began to scrub at his shirt, his grey shorts slung by the weight of water below his belly and his trousers floating beside him like a bubble.

She stared at him and wondered how he could go back to the house before they dried – his clothes, himself. It would be hours before his clothes were dry, even in this heat. She was unable to take her eyes from him.

Suddenly he looked up at her, directly, not searching the hillside but meeting her eyes immediately, and it seemed that she was standing right in front of him with his eyes so yellow, big and frightened.

She looked away from him, at the cottage with its sun porch full of women, then back at him. She drew in breath, and smiled.

The Gift of Maggie

Maggie Hartfield's first sensation that July morning was one of relief – relief that at last the sullen, clinging heat wave had passed. But as she listened to the uneven patter of rain against her window, relief gave way to familiar, helpless anger.

What was she doing in her own bed, at home, on the first day of her vacation? If her husband had taken the time to arrange his holidays to coincide with hers, she might be window-shopping in Vancouver, or relaxing in a cabin in Jasper, instead of feeling grateful that the hot spell in Edmonton had passed so she could do the housework in comfort.

But Fowler could think of nothing but lotteries and horse races. He allowed today to stumble into tomorrow, undirected – always hoping for the best but never planning for it, and then shaking his fist at his blighted fortunes when things turned out badly. They usually did.

The baby was uttering half-remembered adult sounds in his crib, but Maggie permitted herself the luxury of brushing her teeth in privacy before she went to collect him. When she crossed the hall to his room, Timmy pulled himself to his feet and grinned at her. Maggie scooped up the baby and nuzzled her face into his neck. He giggled.

But Maggie barely heard him. Timmy smelled peculiarly medicinal – antiseptic – not at all like his usual clean baby-soap smell.

"If that brother of yours has thrown something into your crib again, I'll have his head," she muttered, pulling off sheets and blankets.

Timmy grinned at her. This was fun. He hadn't seen this much activity in the morning, ever.

Maggie shook the bedclothes, looking for a tube of ointment, a bottle of medicine, anything that might explain the odour. There was nothing. Nor had the sheets and blankets retained the unusual smell. She sniffed Timmy again, and was filled with images of hospitals and laboratories. Timmy began to imitate her sniffing noises, and Maggie laughed as she carried him into the bathroom.

~

When Peter came downstairs half an hour later, Maggie asked him to smell the baby. A bath and clean clothes had done nothing to diminish Timmy's odour.

"Are you kidding?" asked her seven-year-old son. "Before breakfast? No way."

"Oh, come on, Peter. He's clean. Just one little sniff."

Peter shrugged, hiked up his pyjama bottoms, and knelt beside Timmy on the floor.

"Smells okay to me."

"Try again, Pete. Doesn't he smell antiseptic to you?"

"What does that mean?"

"Like disinfectant or something. Like medicine."

"Nope. He smells like Timmy. Are you okay, Mom?"

"Sure I am. Don't worry about it, Pete. I guess my nose is acting up. Come and eat your breakfast."

~

At three thirty that afternoon, Timmy woke from his nap and

pulled himself to his feet. He babbled and called and then stopped to listen, but no one was coming to release him. He bounced up and down on the mattress, enjoying the squeak of the springs and the extra boost they gave his jumps. Still no one came to his door but, to his delight, the slatted side of his crib descended, freeing him, and Timmy tumbled out onto the plush blue rug. He lay still for a moment wondering if he was hurt, and then he saw the open bedroom door and the promise of new places to explore. He smiled and sat up.

Two floors down Maggie, who was folding clothes beside the swishing agitation of the washing machine, felt rather than heard the thump. She looked up. She couldn't imagine what might have caused the brief impulse, and so she assumed it hadn't occurred at all.

Timmy crawled across the rug and through the open door to the top of the stairway. He placed two chubby hands on the corner post and pulled himself to his feet. He grinned at his accomplishment and looked toward the bottom of the stairway for someone with whom he could share his triumph. There was no one. But Peter's shiny new red fire engine was there, unguarded, at the bottom of the stairs. And so, at twenty minutes to four, Timothy Hartfield took his first unassisted step.

He didn't whimper as he rolled and tumbled and thudded his way down the seven stairs, nor did he cry out as his forehead hit the metal edge of his brother's fire engine. Maggie, who had raced up her stairs as quickly as Timmy had toppled down his, was the first to emit a sound.

"Oh, my God," she wailed.

Timmy opened his eyes when he heard the panic in his mother's voice, and then they were both crying – Timmy more explosively, but no more sincerely.

In her state of anxiety, one might think that Maggie would not have noticed the odour of the hospital emergency room. But she did.

~

Fowler stood beside his son's crib for a long time, the anger and frustration licking up inside him until he could no longer contain it. He touched the baby's forehead gently, beside the strip of white gauze. Timmy moved a little in his deep, medicated slumber, but he did not open his eyes.

"Dammit. Dammit." His voice grew louder as he strode out of the bedroom and down the stairs. When he reached the kitchen, he was shouting. "Dammit, Maggie. How could you let a thing like that happen? He's just a baby. He can't protect himself from unfastened cribs and unprotected stairways."

"It was an accident," Maggie said flatly.

"Some accident," he said. "I call it negligence." Fowler banged his fist on the table, making the cutlery rattle. "Why do things like this happen to me?"

"To you?" Maggie whirled around. "I'm as upset about this as you are. But it happened, and you can just thank God that Timmy's all right."

"It wasn't Mommy's fault," said a small voice from the hallway – Peter's voice.

Maggie and Fowler looked at one another, embarrassed.

"I have to watch the lottery," Fowler said, and left the kitchen.

The damn lottery, Maggie thought. It's more important to him than Timmy's accident, more important than talking to me, more important than living.

She wiped her eyes with a sleeve before she turned to Peter.

"Does Daddy think you did it on purpose, Mom?"

She kneeled to him.

"No. He knows it was an accident. Sometimes when we're angry we say things we don't mean. He'll be okay now that he's blown off some steam. Now, go wash your hands for dinner."

~

At seven, Fowler turned off the television, tore his tickets into small pieces, and went to eat his dinner in silence alone. He was more surprised than unhappy that he had not won, because he'd been certain it was his turn.

He wanted to talk about it with Maggie, but she was busy with Timmy, who was awake and miserable. It was not until eleven thirty when she climbed into bed, exhausted, that he had a chance to speak to her. Even then, it was she who spoke first.

"Fowler, there was something strange about Timmy's accident."

He stared at her. "What was strange about it?"

"I smelled it before it happened."

Fowler studied her face for a moment. "You what?"

"I smelled it," she said more quietly. "Timmy smelled like a hospital all day. He doesn't now."

"Oh, come on, Maggie. That's impossible. Maybe you just had a hunch something was going to happen. I get them all the time."

It was true. Fowler had hunches about every horse race, every lottery, even the dream home at the Exhibition. Nothing made Maggie angrier than Fowler's hunches.

"Yours never come true," she said.

"But they will. Someday they will, I just know it. I'm going to win big, Maggie, and we'll be on easy street. Neither of us will ever have to work again."

"I like working, Fowler."

"Sure you do," he said, resting his head on his hand and looking at her. "You earn twice as much as I do, and you don't have to drive all over the city all day trying to sell vacuum cleaners to people who don't need them."

"You could have any job you wanted, Fowler, if you'd give it some effort. You're still young, and you have a fine mind. But you don't want to work for anything. You want diamonds and thousand-dollar bills and dream homes to fall out of the sky."

She immediately wished she hadn't said it.

Fowler switched off the light and then in the darkness asked her softly, "Do you think I'm lazy?"

"No, I don't. But I do think you waste your energies on the wrong things. You know the odds against winning one of those lotteries?"

"Sure I do. But someone's got to win it. Why not us?"

Maggie laughed. "You'd make a great advertisement. Do what you want to Fowler. I'm sorry I blew up: it's been a long day."

She curled up next to her husband and closed her eyes, leaving him wide-eyed in the darkened room to dream of the sleek silver Mercedes and the sun-sprinkled vacation in Tahiti that he knew would someday be his. He'd decided long ago that his first purchase after he won the lottery would be the biggest bottle he could find of Cercle D'Or, the expensive perfume that Maggie loved.

When at last Fowler slept, he was smiling.

~

On the Saturday before Maggie was due to return to work, she smelled gas as she was washing the breakfast dishes. Neither Pete nor Fowler could smell it, but Maggie was determined.

"You can't lose anything by taking the boys over to your mother's house for a couple of hours while I get the gas company to check. Please."

Fowler agreed at last, and Maggie sighed with relief as he loaded the boys into the station wagon and drove away.

The tall blue-uniformed man from the gas company shook his head at her. "No gas leak here, Ma'am."

"But I can smell it. Are you certain?"

"Yes, Ma'am. This needle would shoot way over here if there was leaking gas." He pointed at the portable gas detector, which he had placed on the basement floor. "The nose can play tricks with us, you know. When a fire alarm goes off by mistake in a building, half the tenants think they can smell smoke. Don't feel bad, Ma'am. Happens all the time."

The needle on the machine was frustratingly still. To Maggie, the fumes were nauseating.

"Maybe your gadget isn't working."

He shook his head again. "Sorry, Mrs. Hartfield," he said, reading her name from the card he held in his hand.

He was about to lift the strap of the machine back to his shoulder when the needle began to move – slowly at first, then more insistently, over the dial.

He turned the gas off at its source, studied the pipes, and at last tapped lightly on a joint. It cracked.

"Good God," he said.

Maggie raised an eyebrow at him.

He smiled. "Beats me how you knew about it before it happened."

~

Plumbers are not cheap on weekends, and Fowler was dismayed at the cost of the repair. He was well into a monologue about his bad luck when Maggie stopped him.

"Your luck wasn't all bad this time," she said. "If I hadn't known about it before it started, it might have been much worse."

"Your nose knew, eh?"

Maggie nodded.

Fowler stared at her for a long moment, stood up, paced back and forth across the rug. He rubbed his chin, and then stared at her again. Suddenly he looked at his watch, then grabbed her hand.

"Come on, Maggie. If we hurry, we can still make the last race at Northlands."

~

Maggie stared at the massive horses as they were led into the paddock. She watched the intent faces of the men and women who encircled them, their eyes darting from horse to racing form, from racing form to jockey. What good was a nose against experts like these?

Her husband nudged her and winked. "Okay, baby. Smell me a winner."

"I feel ridiculous sniffing at horses," she whispered.

"It's your theory, Maggie. Here's your chance."

"Maybe it won't work."

"I'll give you a hint. Sniff especially hard when number three comes by. That's Lucky Lady, the favourite. Does that help?" He grinned at her.

Maggie tried to sniff as unobtrusively as possible as the thoroughbreds walked by her. They all smelled like horses, and that was not Maggie's favourite scent.

"Here she comes," Fowler hissed. "Here comes Lucky Lady." His voice was high with excitement, his eyes riveted on the tall, glistening horse.

Maggie thought for a moment that Fowler was right, for as Lucky Lady passed her, she began to receive the faint odour of something not yet identifiable, but pleasant. What was it?

As the powerful hindquarters moved by her, she knew.

Roses.

She turned toward Fowler, her eyes glinting with pleasure and then with surprise. The scent was growing stronger by the moment. It was not coming from Lucky Lady at all, but from the roan mare behind her. The sweet scent was overpowering.

"Can't you smell it, Fowler?"

"Smell what?" He was still watching Lucky Lady.

"Roses. It's number seven. She's the winner."

Fowler consulted the racing form and the mutuels board. He looked at her with amused disappointment. "Sudden Jade? You must be kidding. She's running at twenty-five to one, Maggie. She hasn't a hope."

"Sudden Jade is going to win. The whole aim of this outing was to prove or disprove my ability to choose a winner, Fowler. I'm telling you, number seven is going to win."

He patted her shoulder. "I'll tell you what. I'll put a two-dollar show bet on Sudden Jade. But this twenty goes on Lucky Lady to win."

He waved the bills at her and threaded his way through the crowd to place his bets.

~

In the last race at Northlands that afternoon, with the Ferris wheel rotating unnoticed in the distance, Sudden Jade came from behind in the last lap of the race to beat Lucky Lady – by a nose.

Fowler was smiling as he tore his win ticket to tiny pieces and allowed the wind to carry them away.

"Do you know what this means?" he said, his voice tense with excitement. "You and I are about to make our fortune."

He hugged her and led her in a few dance steps on the way to the cashier's window. People were looking at them, but Fowler didn't seem to notice. He collected his winnings, and then took Maggie by the elbow and led her to the exit.

"We can make a killing here at Northlands alone," he said as they walked. "But I want to do this right. I want to think about it, and approach it from the proper angle. Oh, Maggie, this is the break we've been waiting for." He could talk about nothing else for the rest of the day.

On Sunday morning, his eyes red from lack of sleep, Fowler emerged from the den with a stack of loose-leaf papers in his hand. "I've decided, Maggie," he said. "We're going to start with the lottery."

She looked at him. "Did it take you all night to decide that?"

"Nope. Take a look at these." He handed her the papers. "I've been thinking about how to invest the money. I did some reading about real estate and securities, and I worked out the relative interest rates. Things like that."

Maggie looked over the pages of neat writing. "You've been busy."

He smiled. "Working on this is a hell of a lot more fun than selling vacuum cleaners. First thing tomorrow, I'm going to drive you down to smell the lottery tickets at Southgate."

"I have to go to work tomorrow."

"Don't you realize how important this is, Maggie?"

"I'm sorry. I have a board meeting from nine until noon."

"Then I'll pick you up at twelve."

She nodded and sighed. "All right, Fowler."

~

At a quarter after twelve on Monday, Maggie followed her husband to the lottery kiosk in the shopping centre. There were several people ahead of them, and Fowler tapped his foot with impatience. At last, only an elderly gentleman stood between them and the salesgirl. The man couldn't decide which ticket to buy.

"It's for my daughter," he explained. "She's all on her own now, with three kids." He looked apologetically at the salesgirl, then at Fowler. He moved from foot to foot as he examined the tickets, and Maggie could feel her husband's irritation growing. At last, Fowler grabbed the book of tickets from the old man's hand and pulled one out.

"Take this one," he said.

The old man smiled at him. "Do you think this is it?"

"Sure I do." Fowler had a sudden thought. "Just a minute." He held the ticket under Maggie's nose. "Should the gentleman buy this, or should we?"

She shook her head at Fowler. "He should. It's okay."

The man fumbled through his wallet for the money, and at last was gone.

Maggie pretended to study the fine print on each ticket, inhaling as deeply as she could. But they all smelled the same, like paper. She shook her head at Fowler and they thanked the surprised sales girl and left.

On Tuesday, Fowler drove Maggie to Edmonton Centre and on Wednesday to Meadowlark. For two weeks, Fowler met Maggie each day at noon, and took her to a different location. Each time she sniffed the tickets and shook her head. She had cancelled four business luncheons so far, and her patience was wearing thin.

So was Fowler's. When he picked her up on the day of the lottery, he said irritably, "You can't tell me that there is not one lucky ticket in this whole damned city."

Maggie shrugged. "If there is, I can't smell it. And this is the last try, Fowler. I have more important things to do."

"Okay. We'll give it one last chance."

Maggie failed to smell a winner, and Fowler chose two tickets that "felt" lucky.

That evening, after Fowler had shredded his tickets into the waste paper basket, he sat down beside Maggie on the couch. "Maybe we should try the horses again."

She shook her head. "I don't think there's much point."

"I guess you're right," Fowler said sadly. "It sounded wonderful at the time, but things like that don't really happen, I guess."

"I did predict three events accurately," Maggie said, putting down her book. Her voice was not defensive. She was simply stating a fact.

"It was coincidence."

"I know you're disappointed, Fowler. I'm sorry."

"Don't be. I'm still odds-on favourite to win something soon." He smiled at her, and pulled gently on a strand of her hair. "The only thing I regret is that little investment business we might have had. I got a real kick out of doing all that research."

"Other people make investments, Fowler. They need advice."

"I've been thinking about that. Maybe I'll take some courses." He stood up and pulled his sweater on over his head.

"Where are you going?"

"Down to the club. I haven't played racquetball since this whole thing started. I'll see you later." He kissed her on the forehead and left.

Peter came down to the living room as Maggie watched Fowler drive away.

"Daddy didn't win the lottery, did he?" asked Peter, coming to stand closer to her. "Was he mad?"

"No, Pete. Just a little disappointed. But it's okay, because he's about to win at racquetball."

"How do you know that?"

"I don't know. Maybe it's just his turn. Go on up to bed, Pete, and I'll be there in a minute."

Alone in the living room, Maggie took from the pocket of her sweater a tiny bottle of Cercle D'Or, empty now for months, too expensive to replace. She uncapped the amber bottle, sniffed, and smiled.

There it was, the fragrance she could never forget – the wild, tantalizing scent of a winning lottery ticket.

The Milk Wagon

Buchinski was my teacher, but he was also Mother's lover. Not at the same time. He was my teacher when I was in grade eight, and Mother's lover when I was in grade nine. If it hadn't been for me, for the mutual back-slapping of a parent-teacher interview, they probably never would have met.

I can separate two Buchinskis, one from the other. The one who taught me math was stern and unyielding and disliked me because I knew his ineptitudes. When he made errors on the board – he taught us math and couldn't spell – I pointed them out to him. In return, he inaugurated The Challenger, one intricate problem appended to the Friday math test which was particularly intended to stop me up. When I handed in my paper, his eyes went to it immediately and it was the greatest satisfaction of my week to watch his disappointment when I'd got it right again.

Math was my weak area. I had to study for the tests themselves, and to pay Harold Jenkins ten cents, my allowance, to use his stolen key; each Thursday afternoon he copied down The Challenger from the master on Buchinski's desk.

The Buchinski who visited my mother was another man entirely, and it was partly because she, sewing hems and buttons at the cleaner's all day long, thought a teacher erudite by definition. Buchinski liked to expose the cracks in her knowledge and then to mortar in the chinks, explaining carefully and patiently. She was a better student than I, eager, impressed, and pleased when she'd gained a toe-hold on some concept like Interest and Principal over Time. At home, Buchinski was warm and cajoling with me, as though we would put the unfortunate experience at school behind us and become comrades in the education of my mother. We would, in short, overlook his spelling for her sake.

She was tall and gaunt, her skin pale always as though her later illness had been in the blueprint from the start, but attractive in spite of that. Sometimes when she looked away, daydreaming, there was a mystery to her, some puzzle which she could neither solve nor phrase. This rare expression, withdrawn but more becalmed than concerned, irritated Buchinski.

"A penny for your thoughts," he'd say, and he was dissatisfied when she'd turn him away with a shrug, and smile. But there wasn't much he could do about it.

Buchinski was thick throughout and florid, red-haired with heavy dark eyebrows which added to his air of disapprobation in the classroom but which, when he was trying to be pleasant, raised themselves into a single hairy line – as though he'd tried to glue a moustache over his mouth, and missed.

~

There's no rush. The funeral doesn't start till one. But at eleven-thirty I board the bus which will take me to West's funeral home downtown. It's March and the leaves, pressed by snow all winter, have dried back into September-likeness, and they scud about in the chilly wind. Mother's funeral, orchestrated like Buchinski's by Norman West, was on a brilliant day last August; a more appropriate day than this, one which radiated death through its silken waves of heat.

I spent days sorting and packing away her things, vacuuming and polishing until the room she'd died in was a guest room once again. That wasn't what I'd intended: I'd been looking for comfort in domestic industry. But I'd found none. Nor have I found much since.

The bus has travelled more quickly than I'd expected and it's not yet twelve o'clock when I get off at Market and St. Clair. As I cross into the park across from West's clean, white oblong building (an eddy of shredded leaves the only disorder on his property), the streets are filling with people on their lunch breaks.

I envy their having to be somewhere again at one, the purposefulness of their steps even when they're heading out for food and an hour's relaxation. My lunch breaks are long, directionless, and now I think even of Mother's job as something to be coveted. She had a reason to get up. I have to invent mine: I must call Goodwill so I will clean the cupboards, or be at the museum by ten for a lecture on air-layering plants which I will never put to use, or attend the funeral of a man I haven't seen in twenty-seven years.

They were contemplating marriage. I think my intuition told me that they would when she came back from the parent-teacher interview. Widowers and widows don't meet often even in a city of this size. It took them more than a year to catch up to my intuition, and Mother was shy about it with me.

What I knew of sex I'd discovered on my own, and what I knew of love was not the word of it but the sense she'd given me of the man who was my father. He died when I was two, and I think that having spent so many hours teaching me to know him made her feel awkward admitting a similar emotion toward Buchinski. She also knew I didn't like him: she was cleverer by far than he.

However it was, she sent the two of us out together so that he could broach the subject with me. Having spent many hours with my ear to the air vent in the room above the living room, I knew already that he was determined and she was not yet quite.

When I say he was her lover, I do not intend any sense of

impropriety. If they showed passion, if they were even capable of it, it was not when I was around, assumed asleep or otherwise.

We walked toward the centre of the town. It was a Friday morning during early summer and Mother had taken a week from work to spend some time with me. I knew that she planned another week in late September, and that Buchinski wanted to take that week off to marry her.

"It would be a big adjustment for her," Mother had said to him. "We've been on our own for years."

"What you want is what's important, Lilly," he answered her. He had no children but his students, and those he likely viewed as adversaries when he thought of them at all. "She'll grow up and start a family of her own. They'll be more important to her than you'll ever be."

She would have shrugged at that, I think.

So as we walked in the jade morning, silent and (he obviously thought from the complacency, the damnable assurance of his low round face) companionably, I was already weighing the matters he planned to introduce. I thought of having him in the house more frequently than now, this man whose present stride was bombast. I tallied that against the possibility of having Mother at home when I returned from school each afternoon.

I was at that straddling age, as my elder son is now, where I longed for more time with her than I ever seemed to have, but only when I was away from her. Now she was at home on the pretext of getting the ironing done before the heat while she sent Buchinski and me out to decide her future. In her absence, I could envision our perfect afternoons: her meeting me with new-baked cakes and time to listen, and my telling her the things I never would, should she ever really be there.

With Buchinski strolling along beside me, clearing his throat every half block in preparation for the speech he'd prepared, with my knowing what it was but never giving him an adit to begin, I fantasized a union of my mother and myself in which he was merely the facilitator.

There were maple keys on the sidewalk and the street had an air of satisfaction. Those who had to had already tucked themselves into offices where they indolently fingered papers, fans strategically placed to cool them, or had gone stoically to sit at sewing, tanning, bottling machines that contributed heat to a day that wouldn't take much more of it.

The rest had not yet stirred, or had stirred early to bake or vacuum and were relaxing now, not yet enervated by the day. Behind us came what seemed to me the embodiment of that kind of cataleptic morning: the clopping of a horse and wagon.

I turned, edged part way out of my reverie by the sound. I still recalled the ice-carts, the other horse-drawn vehicles of my memory, but now all that remained of the equine transportation era in our city were the milk wagons.

"Nice old beast," Buchinski said, his phlegm-clearing finally ended by another topic. "Looks like a thoroughbred, that one, though I doubt she'd be pulling a milk wagon if she was."

I despised his usage in silence and watched the horse, tall brown and gleaming, dappled where the sun hit her through the leaves. She didn't look back at me but straight ahead, walking easily, her blinders black leaves cupped against her long brown temples. There was a white mark, not quite a diamond, high on her forehead.

She stopped in the middle of the road, agreeable to stopping, reined by her white-jacketed driver who leapt easily down and angled across the street, his left arm out to balance the weight of the metal basket of milk bottles in his right. The horse slowly leaned her head into her feedbag, tentative, uninterested, then straightened, looking forward.

I turned back, expecting to have to walk quickly if I wanted to catch up with Buchinksi, but he'd paused and as I walked past him he paced himself to me.

"What a life, eh? Clopping down the road with a feedbag always ready?" Buchinski laughed and cleared his throat again. "Slow down," he said. "I want to talk to you."

I slowed. "About?"

"About your mother." He was walking beside me again and I wasn't looking at him, but I knew he wasn't looking at me either.

"What about my mother?"

He took a deep breath, and I could smell his sweat. His big grey teacher's suit, his shirt, all of him was redolent with the acrid, unfamiliar man-smell. The presence of him, larger even than he was, spread into my territory.

"When you get older," he said, "you'll understand it better, but for now you'll have to accept this: I'm going to marry her."

"Did she say yes?" My heart started and I turned to look at him, afraid that I'd missed some split-second of their conversation and that she'd made up our minds already. But I was gratified by a look from him that I'd seen before at the end of math exams.

"She will."

Clop. Clop. Despite my determined pace, the horse and wagon were catching up with us, passing us. I watched the strength of the horse's haunch as she moved forward, always forward, step by step, was reined and stopped. Buchinski seemed to have forgotten the milk wagon, seemed unaware of anything but us.

"It'll be better, you see?" he said intently. "I earn a great deal more than she does, and you know mathematics...." He laughed uncertainly. "You can see what that will mean to you: nice new clothes, movies when you want to go."

I could see that, certainly. The horse clopped, again behind us. Ahead, in the next block, was the beer factory, an immense square of brick almost two stories high with a small tap at knee level on its sheer side, which today had a watering hose and sprinkler attached to it. When I was younger, I'd wondered if that faucet were where the beer came out.

Behind the factory, slicing twice the road we were walking along, were the railway tracks and, as I looked at the sun-beaten expanse of that industrial complex, a sound of which I'd been only dimly aware righted itself in my head as a slow black engine. Dwarfed by the brick building into whose shadow it seemed now to slink, it nosed through the shimmering waves of heat.

"I'm more strict in class than is my nature," Buchinski was saying. "I wouldn't be so strict with you."

I said nothing, watching the train as one box car after another followed the engine across our paths and disappeared behind the building. We'd have to turn left at the corner – or cross the street if we wanted to go right.

"You know," he said, his voice suddenly clearing as though the subject had been changed, "do you know that people buy gifts to celebrate a wedding? Usually they buy them for the…" he paused, "people who've married one another. But in this case, I'd like to buy you a gift for the wedding." He smiled, stopped, turned, his face red and wet as he leaned toward me. "I'd like to buy you anything you'd like to have." His teeth were very white.

I looked down at the sidewalk, shifting my black oxford-shod, white-socked feet, unable to move forward because of the sweating bulk of him before me.

"Anything. The prettiest dress. A doll. Whatever you want, to celebrate."

I thought him stupider than ever, but I wasn't going to let him know that because my mind had been set for some time on a radio of my own – an impossibility on Mother's budget. But instead my eyes went past him to the milk wagon and I said, "Mr. Buchinski, would you buy me a horse to celebrate?"

He looked unsettled as he turned to glance at the milk wagon. The driver was returning to it once again, stepping up as I waited for Buchinski to answer. His back was to me still and I thought I'd have to read his response in his posture because the train, brakes screaming, shunted steam and sound like hot thunder down our street.

The horse's head was up, ears forward, as the driver gave his signal with the reins and she startled suddenly at his order as though, transfixed by that screech of iron wheels, she'd been unaware of his return. She continued to move ahead too quickly toward the intersection and the driver pulled hard back on the reins. But that seemed to irritate her further, to urge her on to a canter, the traces hitting the backs of her hind legs prodding her, faster yet. Blindered to her final exits, she ran straight through the intersection and pounded toward the slow rust boxcars of the train.

"Don't look," I heard Buchinski say, two thin notes behind me.

At the last moment, the driver leapt from the cart and rolled into the dusty street; the horse reared, sensing the rush of air beside the moving wall too late, impelled forward still by the milk wagon she could not outrun. Her neck seemed to hit first, twisting hard left with the motion of the train as her massive chest hit the edge of the car, her head high; her forelegs caught before the steel and pound of the train which would not stop but only screamed and screamed and screamed.

I ran, back through the streets for home with the puffing of Buchinski behind me, until I left him far behind. At the corner near our house I ran left instead of right to the deserted schoolyard. I sat in the hollow of the stairwell by the girls' entrance, my face against the hardness of my knees, my thighs on the coolness of cement. I would not go back until my mother was alone.

~

At five to one I walk up the stone steps of the funeral home and through its open door. I've watched the people arrive – there are many more than came to Mother's funeral, but she was ill for far too long and the circle of her friends diminished.

Buchinski's casket is still open and I stand alone beside it. Most of the others have gone inside or are talking quietly near the entrance to the chapel. Mother's casket wasn't open. She didn't look herself.

Buchinski does. He's older, of course, than when I saw him last, but he was one of those people who acquire greyness and lines without acquiring age. He's a completely lifeless embodiment of tanned health.

Inside that head through all these years has been the memory I refused to share with anyone: the death of a blindered animal on a brilliant summer day.

The attendant comes to close the lid, to roll Buchinski away. The newspaper clipping in my purse says, "Superindendent dies at school board meeting."

I leave before the funeral begins, pausing on the steps to look out on the quiet street. The workers of this city are all back at their desks.

Buchinski outdistanced my mother. He might have been with her for more than a quarter of a century, perhaps have eased her fear at dying alone. My house full of family could not do that, no matter what I did.

But why do I try to move the pieces of the past around? It makes no difference what I do with them; they stay put, every single moment wedged precisely where it was, between the one that came before and the one that followed after. This moment will soon be wedged as well, immutable, complete.

I go forward into sudden sunlight, one step after another. What I draw behind me is of my own design.

The Wife

As Klewchuk scored his third consecutive goal, Malcolm Burgess yawned and dropped the second section of the paper onto the rug. "What's for dinner?"

Katy's face appeared over the front page headlines. "You didn't pick up the steaks?"

He studied her, puzzled, for a moment and then looked stricken. "Oh, God. It's our anniversary."

She sighed and swallowed the last of her beer, placing the glass precisely over the damp circle on the end table so that the surrounding dust would be less obvious. "Never mind. I'll order a pizza."

She folded the first section of the newspaper over the grey spot on the couch beside her. "You want another beer?"

"If you're going." Malcolm raised his empty glass toward her in a toast. "We could go out for dinner."

"I'm tired. And you've got marking to do."

He groaned as Katy moved her briefcase from the coffee table to the front hall, where she had to nudge aside a pair of sandals and one galosh before she had room to put it down.

"I'd rather be writing," he said.

"If you'd spend less time writing, you'd get caught up with your marking."

"When the book's published, I'll never have to teach again." Malcolm sighed. "*He Shoots….*"

Katy was certain that the only way Malcolm's novel would ever see the inside of a bookstore would be if he carried the manuscript into one, but she didn't say so. She tossed an empty cigarette package onto the haphazard stack of magazines on the coffee table, picked up the beer glasses, and started for the kitchen.

"How's it coming?"

"'Nother hundred pages ought to do it." He'd followed her into the kitchen and was leaning against the counter.

"Careful," she said. "You'll get grease on your slacks." She had one cold beer in each hand and she pushed the door of the refrigerator closed with a stockinged foot. "Where did I put the beer glasses?"

"Here." Malcolm reached for two glasses behind yesterday's unscraped dinner dishes. He looked away from the lump of cold potato squatting in a puddle of congealed fat.

"How's it going to end?"

He looked unhappy. "I haven't decided that yet. That's just the problem, Katy. I need time to work it out."

Katy ordered the pizza, then came to sit beside him on the couch as the referee dropped the puck to start the third period. For forty minutes by the kitchen clock, and eighteen by the one at the Coliseum, she didn't say a word.

"I can't stand the mess any more," she said quietly at last.

"Right after the game. I'll start on the kitchen and you can make the bed."

"I thought you were going to do some marking." She re-crossed her feet.

"Why don't we try another cleaning company?"

She shook her head. "We always spend hours cleaning up before they get here so they won't think we're slobs."

As the Rangers tied the Oilers, Malcolm folded his arms across his chest and leaned forward.

Suddenly Katy sat up straight, put her feet on the floor, and said, "I've got it!"

"Got what, Dear?" asked Malcolm, still looking at the set.

"What we need is a Wife."

"I've already got one. Did you see that check?"

"No, you don't. I'm talking about roles here, Malcolm. Roles. What *you've* got is a spouse. What *we* need is a Wife."

"Penalty? What in the hell are they talking about? That was a good clean check."

She moved to stand between him and the television, her hands on her hips. He peered around her. She pressed the knob to turn the television off.

"What are you doing? The game's tied!" He came across to turn on the set again, but she held his wrist.

"I'm trying to talk to you."

He stared sadly at the grey screen.

"I am trying to talk to you about a Wife. We need a Wife, Malcolm. She could have dinner ready for us when we came home, pour us drinks, do the laundry.... It would be perfect."

He reached around her and the announcer's voice burst into the room. The game was over. The Oilers had won.

"They scored short-handed, Katy. I missed it." He sounded close to tears. "You go ahead and get whatever you want. Just let me watch the summary."

So Katy went ahead. It wasn't easy, by any means. When she phoned the newspaper to place the ad, the woman at the other end of the line explained that there was no appropriate classification for what she wanted. "How about 'Domestic Employment'?"

"No," said Katy. "We don't want to pay her, for God's sake."

"You want a servant?"

"No. A Wife. A Wife!"

"Well, even if there was such a classification, it would have to read, 'Husband/Wife Wanted.' Equal opportunity, you understand."

"But we don't need a Husband. We're discussing roles here, not gender. Husbands change light bulbs and earn money, and we've already got two of those. We need someone who cooks and cleans and sews." Katy paused to think. "It could be a male, of course, but it has to be a Wife."

The woman at the other end suggested the Personals column and sounded relieved when Katy agreed. They phrased the ad carefully. "Attractive, warm, youngish couple seeks kind, intelligent Wife (male or female). Goal: mutually rewarding, long-term relationship."

Katy was pleased with her ingenuity when the ad appeared, but at the end of the week the only responses had been from a handful of the types she supposed frequented those video peep-show places.

Confident that a Wife would be arriving soon, the Burgesses had paid even less attention to the house than usual. Newspapers, medical journals and magazines were strewn from front hall to back porch, there was not a single clean plate or glass in the entire house, and the anniversary pizza box on the kitchen table appeared to be growing a new pizza.

"This is ridiculous," Katy said. "I've been taking showers at the hospital because the sight of our bathtub makes me ill."

Malcolm nodded miserably.

"How do other people find wives?"

"Meet them places, I guess. Bars, dances, things like that. Ann Landers is always suggesting church gatherings."

"You take the bars, then, Malcolm, and I'll hit a couple of churches. We'll come up with something."

But they didn't. Malcolm reported that none of the women he'd talked to had been interested in permanent relationships: their sights were set on careers and travel. "I feel badly that I only talked to women," he said, "but I just couldn't bring myself to ask a man if he'd like to be a Wife."

Katy understood. Her search had been equally fruitless. The women she'd found in the churches all seemed adequately outfitted with Husbands and Homes already.

Malcolm sighed, stood, and picked his way through the debris to his briefcase in the hallway. "I give up. We'll just have to do the work ourselves, I guess. But first, I've got to get back to my book before I lose my train of thought."

Katy watched him spread his papers on the coffee table, shoving paper plates and flyers absently to the floor to make room for *He Shoots*.... Within seconds, he was hard at work.

~

As it turned out, the Wife found them.

She was selling crocheted pot holders door to door to support herself. Katy invited her in to the vestibule while she went upstairs to find her wallet. When she came back down fifteen minutes later, the woman had one arm full of newspapers and was sorting the shoes in the front hall closet into neat pairs.

She dropped the papers when she saw Katy. "Excuse me, Ma'am," she said. "I just can't help myself."

Katy proposed on the spot.

Lydia proved to be an exceptional Wife. She was strong enough to carry the carpet cleaner and the floor polisher up the stairs one appliance in each hand, healthy enough that she wasn't puffing when she reached the top. She was tall and blond and solidly built: pleasant looking without being beautiful. She preferred crocheting in front of the television set to expensive evenings on the town, and she said nothing when the Burgesses left the top off the toothpaste tube or shuffled the newspaper sections before she had a chance to read them.

Within a month, the house had been cleaned from top to bottom and Katy was growing accustomed to returning from the hospital to chilled wine in a clean glass and the comforting aroma of dinner already in the oven. The clothes were clean, ironed and neatly hung in the closet, and every loose button in the house had been securely reattached.

The only problem seemed to be with Malcolm, who found the transition from total disorder to total organization more than a trifle unsettling. He complained that he couldn't work because every time he got up to go to the bathroom, Lydia re-stacked his papers and dusted the places where they'd been.

"I can't write up here. I'm going to the basement."

"But it's dark down there, Malcolm. And cold. And probably dusty."

"I doubt that it's dusty, and I don't care if it is. I'll take a lamp and a sweater. I'll use the card table. Don't worry about me. Just tell that Wife of ours to stay upstairs, you hear me?"

More and more often he retreated morosely to the basement after dinner and Katy once thought she heard him mutter on his way downstairs, "If I'd wanted a Wife, I would have married one." She decided she must have heard him wrong.

The Wife was such excellent company that Katy barely noticed Malcolm's absences. Lydia didn't appear nauseated when Katy enthusiastically described some surgical procedure and she uttered not a murmur when Katy changed the channel in the middle of a program. She just sat and crocheted.

Just after Thanksgiving, Katy noted with consternation that Lydia's crocheting was taking on new and alarming dimensions. The project she was sewing together now was already as large as the living room couch and the stacks and stacks of granny squares began to acquire form as they were attached to one another. She finally discovered that Lydia had crocheted *The Last Supper* in two-ply acrylic orlon with a 4.5 mm hook, and at that point Katy decided she'd better do something.

"That's quite a blanket," she said.

"Yes," replied Lydia, threading a strand of purple wool through a large-eyed needle. "The biggest yet."

"Where in the world did you find the pattern?"

"Made it up as I went along. I'm going to try *The Dinner Party* next. Full scale."

Katy swallowed. "And what are you going to do with this one when it's finished?"

"Sell it. I got five hundred for the last one."

Katy blanched. What had started out as a simple hobby was about to turn into a Career, and Katy knew what that meant. If she wanted to keep the Wife, she'd have to keep her busier.

"We could move to a larger place," she mused.

"Oh, no," replied Lydia. "The nice thing about crocheting is that it folds. I've plenty of room right where I am."

Katy eyed her suspiciously, but her expression softened as she hit on a solution.

"We'll have a family," she said.

~

"I suppose that if you're to become a Mother," Katy said later as Lydia loaded the last of the dishes into the dishwasher, "we'll need a father, too."

"I suppose we will."

"We'd better go get Malcolm."

Katy turned toward the basement stairs, then hesitated.

"No. He won't do. Fathers know how to build model railroads and they wear jeans on Saturdays when they putter in the garage. That just isn't Malcolm. Now a Father wouldn't necessarily need to be a male, of course...." She looked at Lydia, thinking. "Although in this case I suppose he would, since you turned out to be a female. We'll have to advertise."

Lydia shook her head. "I know someone who'd be perfect. He makes the frames for my crocheting."

Katy narrowed her eyes at the Wife, but she said nothing. They'd never discussed fidelity before and there wasn't much point in doing so now.

~

Harold was, as Lydia had predicted, an entirely satisfactory Father. While Lydia crocheted scallops to sew around the collars of her maternity dresses and little things in yellow and pale green, Harold papered the guest room in pastel colours and carved a cradle, afterward giving it two coats of unleaded paint. Katy looked on, approving.

For a long time after the arrival of the baby, life at the Burgess household was pleasant, if a trifle overcrowded. But gradually, Katy became aware that she was seeing far less of Lydia than she was of Harold and the baby. Meals lacked creativity and the ironing was haphazard. Sometimes the dust became visible on the furniture before it was removed. Lydia spent a lot of time in the bedroom, which Katy had attributed to post-partum depression until she realized that the baby was six months old.

She knocked on the door of the bedroom and the Wife and Mother opened it just a crack and peered through. A wisp of pale gold wool trailed from her shoulder.

"What's going on in here, Lydia?"

"Crocheting, Katy. But the light is wrong. Harold and I are going to have to move."

Katy was aghast. "You can't do that! You're the Wife!"

"I'm sorry. I truly am. But I've sold *The Dinner Party* now, and we can afford a place of our own." Lydia shook her head. "It's bigger than I am, Katy," she said. "Crocheting is my life."

~

As Katy approached the card table in the corner of the basement, Malcolm looked up.

"It's perfectly clear how it will end. I can't imagine why I didn't see it sooner. He's going to miss the net."

"You can finish it upstairs now," Katy said. "They're gone."

He shook his head firmly. "It's too clean up there."

"Won't be for long." She ran her finger through the thick dust on the borders of the card table. "I guess it wasn't worth the trouble after all," she said quietly. "They just don't make Wives the way they used to."

Print Dresses

In the dresser of this upstairs room there is hand tatted-lace that once was precisely tacked to necklines of dark dresses so that, when necessary, it could be snipped away and gently squeezed in a solution of pure soap flakes and warm water, then left to dry flat on a towel where the sunlight struck it. The sunlight and the soap have made it yellow.

In a lidded cardboard box in the closet, there are balls of brown string, collected from parcels and rolled newspapers and from the grasses and roads where they were once discarded. The ravelling of these brown strings would cross the yard and the gravel road, would wind through the ditch of Queen Anne's lace and into the rows of hollyhocks across the way, in the garden of my aunts.

I can see my aunts through this upper-story windowpane: they are sitting in two canvas lawn chairs in the shade of their small green-shingled house and they're resting for a moment between the weeding of the vegetable garden and the making of the tea. The lazy nods and dips of their straw sunbonnets do not suggest the intensity of their conversation.

They want me to come out. I've seen them in my garden in the early morning when they supposed I was asleep. I've heard them rattle at my doors and windows. They did not intend, when they handed me the key, that I'd come in and stay.

I didn't intend it either. There are things I should be doing, for my work, my home, for you. There are things I ought to be doing here as well, that I have not yet done.

Stacked on an upper closet shelf in this room, there are dozens of photographs of young and handsome men in suits and ties, of women with lace around their necks. These are people who, like my aunts and my mother, knew how to age with grace and self-respect and not a moment of wasted time.

There is a photograph of twelve young women in identical robes of white: some are kneeling, others standing, two sitting on carved chairs. The women are startlingly beautiful, their hair soft and flowing or caught with hairpins up behind their heads. This is the picture of a graduation class, or the cast of a midsummer play: it's impossible to tell, just as I cannot be certain which of the women is my grandmother.

My aunts would be able to tell me, if I asked them. They probably hoped for that, that I would carry pieces from this house across the way and sit in the shade with them while they disclosed the past. Or that I would call from this upper storey window from time to time, bidding them into their mother's house to explain what I was holding. They would have argued between themselves, and even have called in my mother at some point, to settle the matter. They look for excuses to call my mother back, to draw her back to them. This is their way. They grew up as three.

One of my aunts has spied a weed in the flowerbed beside the lawn and she is kneeling on the grass to pluck it. The other aunt is watching her, or looking beyond her to my front door.

What they intended was that I'd discharge it all within a day or two, taking the things I wanted for our apartment in the city, and packing the rest of it into the boxes which they'd left in the woodshed for my convenience. They assumed I'd clean the house from top to bottom in readiness for the agents and the movers.

They are, my mother and my aunts, too old for such emotional and backbreaking labour as disposing of their mother.

Grandmother's bedroom is sparsely furnished and as tidy as she left it. All it required was a little dusting. The thin coverlet, quilted and nearly white, is folded and tucked to conceal the embroidered linen, to save the bedclothes from dust and light. It's a single bed, austere and high, but I like it better than my double one which made it possible for a man to spend the night.

You spent the night ten times, perhaps eleven, before you finally moved in: you said it would be less expensive for both of us that way. You've spent more than you saved on gifts for me or the apartment, luxuries than no one has a need for, and the waste makes me cold.

On her dresser are the bone-backed brush and mirror which she used so dexterously, one in each hand, one hundred strokes through her thin grey hair each night. From her window, which faces away from the house of my aunts, she saw an open field and knew the spit of snakes in the tall weeds, the sticky cling of cobwebs in the trees. She knew them, but left them, too busy with this house for idle wandering: that was for children, the recollections of her own childhood serving up suggestions of blind man's bluff or hide and seek to bored daughters or, later, to her only grandchild. More often, aggravated by such a word as "boredom," she'd send them out to pinch suckers from tomato plants or to hang the wash, insisting on a hat to keep away the sun.

And silences. She expected that the house would be as silent as it is this afternoon no matter how many of us were in it, as she took her one hour's rest exactly with a black stocking over her clouded eyes to keep out light. And so it was.

I think that you would like to live here, for a while. You'd find this old house picturesque, if a trifle small, and would immediately set to work improving it with vertical blinds and bright, bold wallpaper. You'd find a place for a dishwasher and you'd cover the hardwood floors with acrylic, the roof with cedar shakes. Your radio alarm clock would go on the little painted table beside the bed. The table would have to go eventually. So would the bed.

You'd ask me to stop winding the clock on the mantelpiece downstairs because the bonging out of the quarter hours would drive you to distraction.

My aunts have gone into their house. Even the exasperation of my being shut in here will not keep them from getting their tea by the appointed hour. With it, they'll have a biscuit each and plan their supper of aspic and bean salad and sweet brown bread, baked before noon and left to cool on wire racks on the kitchen table's oilcloth. They will wonder, as they set their table with linen napkins and plates and glasses (as their mother always did) what I am eating here.

At the beginning I ate nothing. There were only dead insects where the cornstarch and flour used to be and I wasn't hungry anyway. But then I found her well used cookbooks that she'd made herself from empty scrapbooks, and her round script was steadier than I'd ever known it. I remembered: johnnycake with sweet apple jelly; a white sauce thick on soft macaroni; last week's buns steamed back into edibility. Beside some recipes she'd glued a black-and-white of the woman who'd shared it with her. Martha Beardsley (Pineapple Upside Down Cake, 1941) wears a black one-piece bathing suit and sits by a grey lake with one hand up to hold her damp hair away from her face.

My grandmother was not the cook that you are, with your pepper steaks and Florentined eggs and kiwi fruit from the market. But she didn't waste a cent.

I scoop tea leaves from the canister and wait for the kettle to whistle. Here by the kitchen door I can see out the front window and also out the back: it's a house constructed for people who watch from kitchens. The clock bongs twice: four-thirty. The office will be emptying of everyone but Jack, who'll have to do my work as well as his. And you'll be contemplating a game of racquetball with Harold, followed by a beer. The beer will make you amorous, and you'll remember I'm away.

In the pantry and then in the root cellar, when at last I thought to look there, I found the sealed jars full of fruit and pickled meats, the flour and the sugar in large glass jars with rubber seals so tight that I despaired of opening them, cans of condensed milk and tubs of lard.

I've learned to use yeast again, and to soak the raisins in milk before I add them to the batter. I've recalled bread pudding. I wish that I had eggs.

I clean my clothes in the morning and myself at night, as Grandmother always did. I wash the dresses and the undergarments on the scrub-board which I found beneath the sink. I leave them to dry on the wooden clothes rack in the bathroom.

I wash my hair in the sink, wringing excess water out before I wrap it in a towel. Already it seems longer, silkier. I iron when it's not too warm. There isn't any urgency to that for her cotton dresses fit me, and she had several. Their prints, small and blue or mauve, suit me better than the things I brought with me from the city, and I've stowed all of them away in my suitcase which is in the front hall closet. I'd like to put it out on the verandah and let the aunts decide what to do with it.

My grandmother eludes me. I've looked for her as I swept her auburn corners, as I dusted her varnished wood. I've peered at the hand which held the pan and moved the flannel cloth, sought the fine grain of her wrist, but I haven't found her. I've stood at the foot of her bed when I rose in the morning and studied the indent in her pillow, but it does not belong to her elegant white head. She isn't here. If she were, I'd take her bird bones against my chest and say that she worked well, that there was a reason for it after all.

I see through the dining-room window that my aunts have been duplicitous. Your small green sports car is grinding slowly down their gravel driveway, raising dust which they'll remove from furniture tomorrow. You've brought my mother with you and, in a gesture you'd never dare with me, you walk around to her door and gently help her out. She greets her sisters with two distant hugs and then all three of the women glance toward this house.

I turn away, the kettle boiling now. I know that they will invite you in for something from their table, at least a cup of tea, perhaps cold fruit and biscuits. They've been curious to meet you. And you, so confident, will win them, and give them reassurances. "She's a woman of her own mind," you'll say. "She'll come out when she's good and ready."

And all the time you'll be pitying their set ways, their narrow-mindedness, their silly printed dresses. You'll contemplate entire generations of women who never knew my liberty.

My grandmother is not here, but there's more of her here than I can clean away. In this drawing room, pale wood recalls darker wood, of pews, and hymnals, and Grandmother straight-backed and alert as she attended to the sermon.

In this kitchen is her stern look when a child asked for a second helping of dessert, or an adult one of sherry.

The even seams of her cotton stockings mount the stairs (a neat darn near the ankle almost invisible), and in this room of hers are the drawers in which she kept her long flannel nightgowns and the spotless cotton undergarments.

I am brushing my hair before the mirror – eighty-nine and ninety. The teal-blue print hangs more loosely on me than it did before. She never filled her dresses, either – when I hear your rapping on the door. While you were drinking their tea, I made certain that the bolts on the door were fast, the sashes on the windows firm. My grandmother did not take security lightly.

I will come out eventually. For a time, until you've seen what I am thinking, I will come out to you. But in this house I've remembered why I feel revulsion when you rest your head on my belly and spill your gold, extravagantly, across the bareness of my skin.

I rummage in the top drawer for a hairpin. I know they're here somewhere. When you've finished knocking, I'll go down to pour my tea.

Honey Cat

Greer has been "missing" for six weeks. Tad left last Tuesday for Rio de Janeiro; he's gone to look for her. He hasn't called, which means he hasn't found her.

Tad believes that Greer is somewhere in Brazil because she said on her last postcard that she might go there after Mexico. She said she wanted to see the rainforests before they were all gone.

I told Tad that was as good a reason as I could think of to expect that she was anywhere but Brazil. She could be in Australia for all we knew. Or India.

"No," Tad said, putting socks and underwear into his suitcase. "No. I've got it all worked out. I know how her mind works."

I was leaning in the bedroom doorway, watching him pack. "No one knows how her mind works," I said.

He stopped packing for a moment, his jogging shoes in his hands. Tad's ten years older than I am – nearly fifty now. His hair's gone completely grey, but he still looks good. Keeps himself in shape. "Listen," he said, "I've got it figured out. If she'd gone anywhere else, she'd have sent another postcard. If not to us, then to Roger." He put the runners in the suitcase. "That's what she's been doing since she left. She says she's going to Toronto, we get a postcard from Vancouver. She says she's going to L.A., we get a card from the Grand Canyon." He pulled open the third drawer of the dresser. "Where's my green bathing suit?"

"With the rest of the summer stuff. Downstairs."

He kept putting things into his suitcase until I didn't know how he was going to get it closed. "Greer's left a trail behind her all the way," he said. "If she'd gone to Austria or India, we'd know about it."

"Australia. I said Australia. Not Austria."

"Does it really matter?"

"You gave her too much money, Tad."

"She can manage it. I know Greer." Now he was looking through the closet. "Where's my grey shirt?" He turned. "You've got to help," he said. "It's almost four o'clock."

So I went over to the closet. I took out the grey shirt and handed it to him. I was wondering how he expected to find Greer when he couldn't even find a shirt that was right in front of him.

He was looking at my face. "Deb," he said, "you know, you act like you don't even care that your daughter's missing."

~

I have no evidence that she's missing. "Missing" is a relative term. To Tad, Greer is missing. To Roger, Greer is missing. Those two are the ones who've defined her absence as unusual, as serious. The only person who truly knows whether Greer is missing is Greer herself. To me, she's just away, again. Still.

It's not as though she's on her own. She was with two other kids when she left Mexico City. Americans. She's probably with them still – admiring the Acropolis or camping on a mountain in Tibet. The world's not a very big place, as far as she's concerned.

Tad's his own worst enemy with Greer. Always has been. No one in his right mind would hand a nineteen-year-old kid a pile of money and tell her to go see the world. First he sends her off, and then he wants to get her back again. Spins her out, and tries to pull her in.

Only string he attached this time was that he didn't want her to go alone. So she took Roger. A typical choice for Greer. She's known Roger five years and a fool can see that he's been crazy about her from the start. But I doubt she's ever let him kiss her. Not even touch her, would be my guess.

Kids are supposed to be more reckless than their parents. Hot-headed and hot-blooded. But Greer's never been attached to people. Even before the cat, she was a loner. Tad never understood it. Took it personally. That just made it worse. From the moment she was born, he was always bringing her things – presents. I knew he was spoiling her, that all that stuff was a mistake. But he blew up whenever I said anything about it.

When she was little, he'd get irritated when she called for me instead of him, when she came to me instead of him. It was like he wanted her all to himself. He couldn't see that she loved him, in her way.

The older she got, the worse he got. He'd bring her a swing set, and then get mad when she didn't want to stick around all afternoon and help him put it up. He'd buy her a radio and be hurt when she wanted to watch the television. He'd explode at her. That made her keep her distance.

I understood Greer better. We were close, in those days. She was a good student, loved music and became an excellent swimmer. She was fairly quiet, shy with other people. Bit of a loner, like I said, but that was all right with me.

Those years weren't perfect by a long shot, but I don't expect life has much to offer in the way of perfection. They were the best years I'll ever get with Greer.

If only Tad had stopped bringing things to her, and expecting her to go crazy with gratitude. He wanted cartwheels.

When she was thirteen, he finally got them.

~

I was cooking dinner when Tad came through the front door from work. I was nearly roasting myself, but I always cooked them proper meals back then. Always a hot meal at dinnertime, no matter what the temperature outside. I don't bother with that any more.

"Greer!" he yelled as he came into the kitchen. "Greer!" I could tell by the tone of his voice it was another present. "Where's Greer?" he said. "She isn't going to believe this."

"Oh, Tad," I said. "Not again."

"I didn't buy it," he said, defensive. He wasn't about to tell me what it was, but he was all lit up with excitement. I remember thinking, she's too young for a car.

I went back to mashing the potatoes, and he went out the back door and started calling for her in the yard.

Just then, Greer wandered into the kitchen. She must have fallen asleep in her room. She still looked tired, and hot.

"What's going on?" she said.

"Your dad has brought you something."

The back door slammed as Tad came back into the kitchen.

"Don't move," he said. "Just stay right where you are." He went out the front way again.

"Now, Greer," I said.

"I know, I know," she said, yawning. "I'll be enthusiastic."

We heard a mewing sound, and in Tad walks with the scrawniest-looking creature I've ever seen in my life. It sounded like a kitten, but it looked more like a rodent of one kind or another. Maybe a ferret.

Greer's eyes had grown wide with delight as soon as she saw it, and now he handed it to her.

"Oh, Mom. Look," she said under her breath, holding the grey kitten in the crook of her arm. It continued its thin mewing.

"What do you think of that?" Tad asked her.

I said, "I don't think…"

"I was talking to Greer," he said lightly.

"It's wonderful," she said. "She's wonderful."

"Good," Tad said. "That's good. You're happy, then?"

"Oh, yes. She's so beautiful. So soft."

I couldn't imagine how anything that bony could be soft.

I said, "We can't...."

"Deborah," Tad said sternly. "Just look at her, will you?"

I looked. Greer's head was down, her cheek against the creature's head. Her eyes were closed and the cat's cries seemed to have slowed a little.

"Best present ever," she said in a sing-song voice. "The best." She walked around the kitchen with it, around and around. Then she said, "Come on, honey cat. I'll show you the rest of your new home."

"Honey Cat," Tad said as she started down the hall. "That'd make a great name." He looked at me, nodding. "Honey Cat. I like it."

"We can't have a cat," I said. "We agreed. No pets."

"This is different."

"How can it be different? We talked about it. We agreed. They're messy. You can't go away and leave them...."

Tad began to pace. "She's lonely. This will give her...."

"She's not lonely," I said. "She's got me. She's got us."

"She has no friends."

"This isn't going to help her make friends. Besides, she's fine."

Like he was in another world, he said, "Did you see the expression on her face?"

"I don't want her to have a cat."

Greer's voice, deliberately small, said, "Dad?" and we turned to find her at the door to the kitchen, still carrying the cat.

"I really love her, Dad. Thank you." Then she looked at me. "I can keep her, can't I?"

"I'll have to think about it," I said.

"Of course you can," Tad said. "Of course you can keep her."

"Mom?"

"Didn't you hear what I said?" he said, looking at me hard. "Besides, I can't take it back. I didn't get it from a pet shop, and I can't take it back."

Greer wanted to know where he did get it, and Tad told her a man at his office had to move and couldn't keep it. The cat was mewing loudly again and the next thing I knew, the two of them had gone off – with the cat – to buy it a dish and a basket to sleep in, and some food. Made no difference that dinner was already cooked, that I'd have to keep it warm in all that heat.

~

That night, I was lying in bed, flipping through a magazine, when Tad came into the bedroom. He was humming as he went into our bathroom and started to brush his teeth. After a minute, he came out with the toothbrush in his mouth.

"You should go have a look at them," he said. "Curled up together, fast asleep."

"Where'd you get it?" I said.

"It's like she's a little girl again, the expression on her face. She looks like a little kid again."

"She is a little kid," I said. "Who gave it to you?"

He went and put his toothbrush away and rinsed his mouth. When he got into bed, he said, "I found it. Sort of." He sighed. "Don't tell this to Greer."

I didn't like the tone of his voice. He'd stopped talking so I said, "Why not?"

"It was tied up, with a hammer, in a sack," he said. "That's why."

"God." I thought of that scrawny creature and I felt sick. "Where?"

"Out near Nisku," he said. "Driving back from Jack Weston's place when this kid comes running up out of the ditch. Nearly ran into him. He was a big fat kid, and ugly. Turns and looks at me, scared like. Big pimply face. I hit the brakes, spun out, gravel shooting everyplace. When I look again, he's gone. The bag's in the middle of the road, but he's disappeared." Tad shook his head. "I could have run right over him, the creep. I could have wound up in the ditch."

"The cat was in the bag," I prodded.

Tad sighed again. "Yeah. I could see the bag was moving. I couldn't just leave it there for him. I couldn't just drive away." He was gone into the memory.

"Why did you bring it here?"

He shook his head. "First I took it to the animal shelter. Filled out papers. Reported the kid. The woman told me the chances of anyone taking it were pretty slim. People want younger kittens. She figures this one's four, maybe five months old. I looked at it lying there, purring, in her lap. That's when I thought of Greer."

"Oh, Tad. It's probably got a disease or something."

He rolled over and turned his back to me. "Cut it out, Deborah. Just cut it out. They checked it over. There's nothing the matter with the cat. You act like you're jealous or something."

"Why would I be jealous?"

He didn't answer for a minute. Then he said, "It's crazy about Greer."

"Tad I'm only concerned about…."

"And she's crazy about it." He clicked off the light on his bedside table. "I've finally brought her the perfect gift."

~

Honey Cat wasn't crazy about me. Knew I didn't want it, maybe. It tolerated Tad, but it was Greer's cat from the beginning. If it had been vicious with Greer or Tad, everything would have been different.

With Greer, Honey Cat was the epitome of Contented Cathood: just seeing her made it purr. But when I went near it, its back fur went up and its teeth were bared and it made a hissing sound. After a try or two, I knew better than to put my hand anywhere near it.

Tad thought it was funny. He thought it was cute, this show of loyalty to Greer from such a small, thin cat. It wouldn't let him pat it, either, but at least it didn't bite him.

Sounds stupid, but I have to admit I was afraid of Honey Cat. I began to avoid Greer's room when she was away at school. The cat would stay there, on her bed, guarding it until she got home. Never came out, even when she left the door open. It would look at me when I came to the door, ears back, wary. If I took a step toward it, it sat up and hissed at me.

"I can't get in to clean," I told her. "Your room hasn't been vacuumed in a week."

"I'll vacuum it. I'll dust it, Mom. You don't have to come in any more."

"But I like to…."

"It's my room," she said in a new, adult-sized voice. "I'll look after it."

She did, too: dusted, vacuumed. And she did everything for the cat – fed it, changed its litter, everything.

What did I want her to do? I must have known that she wasn't going to give it up for my sake. To her, it was simple. If I didn't like her cat, I should stay away from it.

Tad said, "Well, it's making her more responsible."

"It's making her withdrawn," I said. "She comes home after school and goes into her room. She doesn't talk to me any more. The only time I see her is at dinner." I shook my head. "I can't even go in there to kiss her goodnight. That damned cat is tearing us apart."

He told me I was over-reacting and went into the bedroom to prove that I was wrong. After a few minutes, he came back out and smiled at me.

"No problem," he said.

"Not for you."

"Oh, come on, Deb. She loves that cat. That's all that matters. It's not hurting anyone."

"Some day it will," I said. "It's vicious."

"That little thing?" he said mildly, turning on the television set.

~

Its grey and white fur never grew in evenly, and it always looked a little patchy and ragged. By the time it was a year old, it was a little fatter, but it was never an attractive cat: especially with those wary green eyes in slits. None of that mattered to Greer.

"She's happy," Tad kept saying, meaning, I've made her happy. "Leave her be," he'd say. Every night he went in there and kissed her goodnight, just to prove something to me. He would have called it reassurance.

Greer changed a lot in those eight months: she was growing up as well. Her auburn hair was longer, seemed thicker, and her face was becoming finer, more angular. Breasts were beginning, and she seemed more sure of herself physically. "She's gonna be something, isn't she?" Tad said. I wondered what he'd do to the first boy who took an interest.

I could hardly complain about her behaviour. She kept her room – their room, hers and Honey Cat's – spotless. Her marks were excellent. She went to bed on time.

But she'd become so distant. She never started a conversation, only answered when she had to, and in as few words as possible. She spent most of her words on Honey Cat: murmured and chattered behind the closed door of her bedroom. She'd open her window when the cat wanted out, or in. I hardly ever saw her.

It finally became like a stranger was living in my house. Tad could go in and have a little chat with her whenever he wanted to, but if I wanted to speak with her, I had to wait for her to come to me. It seemed like when we did talk, we were always arguing.

It's funny how anger shows up sometimes. I began to detest grocery shopping because I'd have to get food and litter for that damned cat.

~

About a year after Honey Cat arrived, Greer quit her swimming without telling me about it. Her coach called: that's how I found out. I told Greer she had no business doing that without our permission.

"I'm fourteen," she said, cool and acting in her new, superior way. "I can make decisions on my own." Her tone made me even angrier than her words.

"You cannot," I said. "Not as long as we feed you. Clothe you. Put a roof over your head."

"Now, Deborah," Tad said, taking a sip from his beer. "Maybe we should…."

"No, Tad," I said firmly. "I'm not discussing it. She continues with her swimming, and that is that."

"It's not fair," Greer said. "You're acting like a dictator. As usual. I won't go if I don't want to." She turned to her father, looking for support. "Dad…."

"It's that bloody cat," I said. "You were never…."

"Honey Cat's got nothing to do with it."

"It's making you nasty. As nasty as it is."

"Now, Deborah," Tad said. "Maybe we could…."

"What else is going on?" I asked her. "What else haven't you told us about? What other decisions have you made yourself?" If Tad wasn't going to take responsibility for his daughter, I would do it all myself.

"Oh, God," Greer said, rolling her eyes. "Don't be so stupid."

"Now," Tad said. He looked alarmed. "Now, Greer...."

"What did you say to me, young lady?"

Greer just tightened her lips and glared at me.

"Now, Greer," Tad said again.

"That does it," I said. "That does it. I will not have you talk to me like that."

As I headed for the door, Tad said, "Wait, Deborah. Calm down. Greer. We've got to talk about this."

I started down the hall, furious. Greer was right behind me – finally paying attention.

"No, Mom. Please," she said. "I'm sorry. What are you going to do? Please, Mom. Please. Leave Honey Cat alone."

It was up on the bed when I opened the door, its back up, hissing. I swallowed. Hesitated. Went for it. I was going to throw it out, I think. Out into the street.

It attacked. Snarling, hissing. I felt its claws rip down my cheek, my arm. I think I screamed.

I could hear Greer behind me, shouting, scared. "No, Mom!" she was yelling. "No!"

Tad had come into the room and he was yelling, too. "Jesus, Greer! Get it away from her!"

"Oh, God. Oh, God," I said. I straightened, moved back. Turned. I had my hands up to my face. The cat was still making a low yowling noise.

Greer was crying, whispering and crying. "Mom. Honey Cat. Oh, Honey Cat. Oh, no."

Tad took me by the arm and led me down the hall. Behind us, the cat quietened.

"You're scratched pretty bad," he said. "I think I'd better get you to a doctor."

"I told you," I said. "I told you." I couldn't stop saying it. "I told you. I told you. I told you."

~

Tad told Greer to get rid of it. Stupid. Of course she couldn't. Wouldn't. She begged and pleaded with him to let her keep it. But this time, he couldn't ignore it, with those marks on my face.

A few days later, he came home while Greer was at school. He had a sedative he'd got some place. He mixed it up with some tuna fish, and put it in Honey Cat's room. Ten minutes later, Honey Cat was out cold. He threw a towel over the cat and carried it out through the kitchen.

"What are you going to do with it?" I asked him.

"Dump it in a field. Far as I can get from here." He paused. "Do we really have to...?" But then he looked at my cheek and shrugged, embarrassed.

Still he didn't move. He said, "She's going to be furious. Can you tell her it ran away or something? You opened the door and it took off?" He looked down at the package in his arms. "She loves this cat so much."

~

She thought we'd killed it, so I told her the truth. I had to. She didn't come out of her room for two days, except to slam into the bathroom. She wouldn't eat, and she refused to go to school.

I tried to talk to her but she wouldn't say a word. She lay still, her face buried in her pillow, her long hair curling down her back. I touched her arm and she jumped and pulled away.

Everything in her room was clean and waiting. While I'd been out getting groceries – her favourite foods, to tempt her – she'd emptied and refilled the litter box, and put out fresh food and water. Her own lunch, on a tray beside her bed, was as untouched as the cat's. I got up, still uncomfortable in Honey Cat's room, and closed her window. When I went into the hall, I heard her open it again.

Tad tried to cheer her up, too, but he had no more success than I did.

"She'll get over it," I said. "It's a loss, but she'll get over it."

"I just wish it had run away," he said. "Wish it hadn't been me."

~

Honey Cat came back, of course. "The cat came back." It was one of Greer's favourite songs when she was a little girl and the words drove themselves into my head where they stayed and played on and on, over and over, night and day. "It just couldn't stay away."

I told Tad he hadn't taken it far enough. He gave a little shrug.

The change in Greer was instantaneous and immediate. She "forgave" us. She went back to school, started to help around the house. She never mentioned the previous few days. We didn't, either. None of us mentioned Honey Cat. It was as though the cat weren't there, in Greer's room. But it was.

Greer acted as though her life depended on her behaviour. She was trying to be so nice to me that her face took on the hardness of a mask. Tad was the same way. When we were alone, we could think of nothing to say to one another. I waited, and the tension built and built.

One night about eleven, a storm came up suddenly and the wind came scudding down the hall, moaning, banging the door in Greer's bedroom against its jamb. Tad went to tell her to close her window, but there was no one in the room. Greer and the cat were gone. It can't have been the first time the two of them had gone out together to walk at night, but it was the first time they'd been caught.

Tad was out the front door in no time. Didn't even take a jacket. I stood at the window, watching the waving trees, and waited.

Twenty minutes later, they came in through the back door and through the kitchen.

She was screaming at him. "Let go of me! Don't you touch me!"

Tad had her by the arm and she was trying to pull away. He shouted back at her. "I'll touch you if I please! I'm your father!"

Her face was red, her hair wind-blown and wild. "Leave me alone, you bastard!" she shouted. "Leave me alone! I hate you!"

"Stop it! Tad! Greer!" I was shouting, too, but it was like I wasn't there.

"Let go of my arm," she yelled, and finally she twisted away from him. "Leave me alone!" she yelled.

He let her go. She ran down the hall into her room and slammed the door. Suddenly the house was silent. There was just the wind outside.

"She's gone crazy," he said.

"Where's the cat?"

"She chased it away."

That really surprised me. "Where?"

"In the park," Tad said. He looked drained, exhausted, and his voice was quiet now. "That's where I caught up with her. She had it on a leash." He looked at me. "Did you know she had a leash?"

I shook my head.

"Me, either." He shook his head. "Suddenly she sees me. She stops and turns, waits until I'm almost caught up with her. But then she starts to run, cutting across the park, the cat beside her on the leash. I start to run after her, and that's when she lets it go."

Crashes and thumps were coming from Greer's room. She was throwing things. Tad and I acted like we didn't hear a sound.

I said, "Why would she let it go?"

His eyes were on me. "If it hadn't been for that damned cat, she wouldn't have been out there, Deb. None of this would have happened."

"She saw that you were.... She was protecting it from you."

"She bends down. She picks it up and kisses it real fast. She unhooks the leash and puts the cat down on the grass. By then, I'm almost caught up to them again. She starts shouting at it, 'Run, Cat. Run, Honey Cat!'" He closed his eyes. "Chasing it away from me! Chasing the damned cat away from her own father." He opened his eyes and looked at me. "I'm the one who gave it to her."

The thumping sounds continued from Greer's room.

"It stops for a second," he said. "I can see its eyes reflecting in the street light. I take one step toward it, and she yells, 'Stop!' That's when it took off." He took a deep breath. "I took her by the arm, and she went crazy." After a moment he said slowly. "What the hell was she doing out there with it, all alone out there?"

Through the window, out of the corner of my eye, I saw a flash of grey.

"It's here," I said. "It's back."

"Where?" He stepped over to the window, but saw nothing.

"Just shot across the lawn."

Suddenly Greer stopped throwing things. Honey Cat was at her window. We could hear new sounds now; the cat scratching to get in. We heard her talking to it, heard the cat scratching on the window, yowling to get in.

"She's shut it out," I said. "You'd better do something."

This funny look had come over his face, like he was going to collapse or something. He wasn't angry any more. He was something else. Sad? Afraid, maybe. He closed his eyes.

"Are you all right?" I asked him.

"I feel sick," he said. "The whole thing makes me sick. Do something if you want."

"Just go and get it, Tad," I told him. "Go out and get the cat."

"And then what? I can't Deborah. I can't. I would have killed it. Do you understand that? I would have killed the thing she loves the most."

~

The cat scratched off and on until nearly morning, but she didn't let it in. I know, because I was awake all night, and I would have heard that window lift. It was the worst night I've ever spent. Longest, too. Her crying on the inside and talking to it, and Honey Cat yowling on the outside. Yowling and scratching to get in. I wanted Tad to make it stop, but he didn't. He let it go on and on – all that noise and pain.

At one point he did get out of bed, about one o'clock, and I thought he was going to do something at last. But nothing changed, the noise kept on, and after a while I got out of bed and went into the hall. He was sitting on the living room couch, in the dark. Just sitting.

I went toward Greer's door, and knocked on it.

"No!" She was crying. "No!" she shouted. "Go away!"

I said, "It's me." I had my hand on the doorknob, was about to turn it.

"No. Go away. Go away!"

Tad didn't move for hours. Didn't do a thing. If he had, maybe I could have had her back, my Greer. My daughter. But he didn't.

She never let it in. Around five, when it was still dark, the cat noise finally stopped. A few minutes later, Tad went and had a shower. He got dressed without saying anything and then he went outside. After a few minutes I heard the car start, and he drove away. I lay there for an hour, and then I got up and went across the hall.

Greer was lying on her bed, tangled in the bedclothes, head back, fast asleep. Even in sleep her face was drained and sad. I approached her cautiously but she didn't flinch when I touched her. I eased the pillow under her head and covered her up. I pulled down the blind. There was no sign of the cat.

~

We never talked about it. Nothing ever really healed: it just got caked in time. Everything changed that night, particularly Tad. He knew he had no control, I guess. That she could do anything to him. He kept buying her more things, more and more, kept taking her more places than any kid I've ever heard of. Still trying to draw her in.

But Greer will not be drawn in by anyone. She has no idea what it means to be close to people. Doesn't know what loving someone means.

First time she mentioned that cat again was just before she left on this trip. We were sitting in the living room, packing things in suitcases and knapsacks, when she looked up and said, "Honey Cat's still out there someplace."

I was startled. "After all this time?"

"I'm sure she is. I can feel it. Stronger now than ever."

I laughed, trying to dismiss it. "Don't tell me you've been looking for her."

"Are you kidding? You'd probably still try to kill her."

I shook my head. "We were trying to protect you, Greer."

"Trying to protect yourselves."

"No," I said, keeping my voice even. "You were obsessed with that cat. It wasn't healthy."

"You should have just left us alone. Honey Cat and me. We weren't hurting anyone."

"You had no one but that cat."

"You're right," she said. "I didn't."

~

Tad. Tells me to trust him: he knows how to handle her. He doesn't know at all.

And now he's off tramping through rainforests, trying to track her down. I think he really hopes she's missing. That he'll find her. That one more time he'll see her grateful. Happy to see him. He wants to fix what happened.

I don't think she's missing. I think she's just wandered off a little farther. He may not find her, and he may, and whether he does or not will be entirely up to her. One way or another, she'll come back eventually, and stay here for a while. She'll let him think it's erased and finished, and then she'll go away again. Someday she'll go for good.

It's too late. I know that, and so does Greer. It's only Tad who doesn't.

Keeping House

It was never said that Rosalie was expected to visit her uncles every Saturday while her parents were away. On the other hand, while she waited for weeks for her mother to explain what arrangements had been made for them, she never did. The note her mother handed her the day before they left gave instructions on how to pay the bills, and when to water the plants, and what to feed the birds. At the very end it said, "Check on Spenser and Victor once in a while." The key ring in the envelope had a key to their house on it.

Rosalie, dangling the key ring from her middle finger and glancing over the list, told her mother not to worry, that she'd take care of everything. She was rewarded by the expression that had appeared increasingly in the past few years on her mother's usually impassive face: a mixture of delight and gratitude that lifted some years away. It pleased Rosalie to have provoked it. At that moment, it was worth a few Saturday afternoons.

She had tickets to the opera the first Saturday after her parents flew to London, so it wasn't until the second week that she was able to visit her uncles. Having no sense of whether they expected her to simply arrive on their doorstep nor whether they were put out that she'd missed the week before, she phoned before she went. Spenser sounded genuinely surprised to hear that she was coming, but he didn't tell her not to. She was surprised as well. She'd been certain they were expecting her.

Although they were her mother's brothers, Victor and Spenser seemed to be from an earlier generation. Her mother had been born ten years after Spenser, which made Victor nearly eighty. Spenser was the stronger of the two, tall and thin. Victor, stooped and unsteady as he was, was more compact and looked heavier. His skin was smoother, lax in places, spotted with brown. Aside from their physical differences, they'd always seemed very much alike to Rosalie: they were two taciturn old men she barely knew at all.

They lived in the dark two-storey house downtown where they'd lived since they were born, except for the years when they'd been overseas fighting in the war, and a brief period later when Spenser had moved elsewhere because he was married. After less than a year, the woman he'd married had gone to live with another man, in another city, and Spenser had moved back home. This happened before Rosalie was born, and she hadn't been told about it until she was nearly twenty.

Since Rosalie's grandmother had died, many years ago, Rosalie's mother had been going over there for a few hours every Saturday afternoon. She'd clean the house and make dinner for Rosalie's uncles, and occasionally she'd stay and eat with them. Even more occasionally – two or three times a year – Rosalie's father, and Rosalie herself when she was still at home, would stop by at six o'clock and eat some of the dinner, too. These meals were not prepared the way her mother usually did them: the vegetables were softer and the meat less tender. They reminded Rosalie of her grandmother.

The uncles were so quiet, so thoughtful and curious of countenance but so quiet, that Rosalie used to imagine them retiring onto a shelf when they were not being visited, needing someone at the door to make them real again. The vision was ridiculous, of course. They worked in their garden, and went for walks, and attended church. Until arthritis crabbed up Victor's hands, he'd built things –

birdhouses and cedar flower containers. And until not so many years ago, Spenser had got up every morning and gone off to work in the offices of the telephone company.

~

Rosalie's mother had been determined to start her first and perhaps only trip to Europe – her trip of a lifetime, she'd called it once – in England, in April. Rosalie thought that was a little corny, but she didn't begrudge it. She begrudged her parents nothing, except – she discovered, as she walked up Victor and Spenser's front sidewalk on that wet and chilly afternoon in early May – having left the uncles behind. She rang the bell, feeling like their cleaning lady.

Victor answered the door and looked up at her as though he wasn't sure what to do with her. He was older and even more stooped than the last time she had seen him. His loose jowls hung nearly to his collar, and he leaned on a cane for balance. She smiled and greeted him, and he stood aside to let her in.

He was wearing a paddy-green cardigan over his shirt and his baggy grey trousers, and soft bedroom slippers over dark socks. He had always dressed this way at home, formal and informal at the same time, and she was conscious of her frayed jeans and bulky sweatshirt and the bandana over her hair. Work clothes seemed inappropriate here, despite the fact that she had come to work. He waited patiently as she took off her overcoat and her rain boots and put her umbrella in the stand.

He led her into the living room, where Spenser rose, putting a folded newspaper down on the seat behind him. He was also carefully dressed.

"Nice of you to come by," he said.

Victor said behind her, without enthusiasm, "I'll make some tea."

"Can I help?" she asked.

The men exchanged glances, then Spenser shook his head. "Victor can make the tea. You have a seat." He indicated the hard-backed couch in front of the picture window with a gesture. He had long, thin fingers, and the gesture was unexpectedly graceful.

She went and sat down on the couch, and Victor went off toward the kitchen.

The house was dark from the greyness of the day – lights were on – but in the afternoon's dimness she saw that the place was not untidy. The week's newspapers were stacked neatly beside Spenser's armchair, and magazines and books were carefully arranged on the coffee table. There was a fine coating of dust on the furniture.

She crossed her ankles, aware of her socked feet.

"How have you been?" she asked.

"We've been fine," he said, nodding several times. "We've been fine."

He, too, crossed his feet, and cleared his throat. He'd leaned back into the Naugahyde and plaid fabric of the armchair, but he didn't look relaxed. His hands were square around the ends of the armchair. He leaned forward a little again. "Have you heard anything?"

"Anything? Oh." She shook her head. "No, not a word. They must be…."

From the kitchen came the sound of something clattering to the floor: a clatter, not a smash. Rosalie looked at Spenser, wondering if she should go and help, but he was looking at her intently, waiting for her to continue.

"Maybe I should go and help him."

Spenser shook his head and indeed, at that moment Victor appeared in the hall with a heavily laden tray. He looked as though he too feared he'd drop it, he was concentrating so hard on it and moving so deliberately. He'd left his cane in the kitchen of course; it seemed impossible that he would make it safely all the way into the living room. She stood and moved toward him.

"I'll manage," he said tightly.

Rosalie cleared a place in the middle of the coffee table, then watched apprehensively as he neared the edge of the rug. But he stepped heavily over the fringe and finally lowered the tray onto the end of the table: shaking a little and huffing.

Rosalie sat down at the opposite end of the couch from where she'd been seated earlier, and Uncle Victor carefully came around and took his seat beside her. With one hand still gripping the tray, he leaned forward and pushed some books aside. Rosalie held her breath again. The whole undertaking was as precarious as a house of cards. But he slid the tea tray safely onto the table so that it was directly in front of him.

Spenser, who'd watched all this in silence, apparently undisturbed, said in a voice in which she heard a well gnawed worry, "She hasn't heard from them either."

"No news could be good news," Victor said.

"Of course it is," Rosalie said. "I didn't expect to hear from them yet; they haven't been gone very long."

Both men were looking at her.

"You know how long postcards take…." She hadn't even considered that her parents might not be having a wonderful trip.

"We've been to Europe," Victor said.

"It's not a pleasant place," said Spenser, nodding. "It isn't safe."

"But you were there during the war."

"It's the kind of place that has wars."

"You've never been there," Victor added firmly. "We have."

After a few moments more, he lifted the teapot and poured the tea. Rosalie got up and handed Spenser his cup, and offered him a biscuit from the small plate. He shook his head, and Victor didn't take one either. Rosalie did. They were stale and hard.

From her new location on the couch, she could see the dining room, which was also clear of clutter. A vase of wilting flowers stood on the dining room table. The lengthening silence – as they sipped and Rosalie chewed – was increasingly discouraging. How did her mother do this? How did she begin?

She leaned forward to put the cup down on the table, and as she did, something – the click of the cup against the saucer, a musty scent – brought her an image from a visit long ago. She remembered her mother, much younger than she was now, coming into the archway of the dining room to tell them that dinner was ready. Her mother had been dressed for dinner: she'd worn a dress, and stockings, and pretty black shoes.

Rosalie glanced down at her jeans with discomfort. Her mother never came here casually dressed, even though she came to clean. Rosalie pulled her feet back toward the couch.

"How are you?" Spenser asked suddenly.

"Fine. Fine. Thank you." She moved a little, re-crossing her legs. The couch was hard and uncomfortable: too short from stem to stern.

He said nothing more, and Victor continued to drink his tea in silence. She wondered if the ability to converse grew moribund from lack of use.

"Work's been busy," she said. "Busier than usual." She was marshalling excuses for future absences, and she knew it. She was not proud of her herself.

"It's good to have a job," Victor said, stressing the word "have."

"Oh, yes, it is. I wasn't complaining," she said.

Victor offered them more tea, and Rosalie accepted and again assisted with the collecting and dispensing of the cups, the offering of milk and sugar, the passing of unaccepted biscuits. Her spirits continued to decline.

She insisted on carrying the tray back to the kitchen, and Spenser followed her. The sink could use a scrubbing, and there were a few crumbs and what looked like a streak of gravy on the glossy white surface of the table. She put the tray down on the counter and turned to Spenser.

"I came to help," she said, indicating her work clothes.

He smiled and shook his head. "I always clear up after tea. It's our system. Victor does the preparation, and I do the cleaning up."

"But the other things. The vacuuming and dusting...."

Gently he said, "Don't worry about us."

As she went out through the hall, she saw that Victor had nodded off in his seat on that most uncomfortable couch. If her mother had been here, Rosalie would have shouted at her.

~

She called the following week, on Sunday, and Spenser sounded almost cheerful. A postcard had come from England and they were feeling reassured, although Spenser pointed out that it had now been more than two weeks since the postcard had been sent. As she continued to coax him through the conversation, he said they'd been out working in the garden every day all week.

She determined not to worry about visiting them. They were doing fine without her, and it was not as though she was short of things to do.

~

When Rosalie heard her father's voice on the phone, she was immediately alarmed: her father hated to use the telephone.

He was calling to say that her mother had been in a hospital in Dover for two days with food poisoning. Now that the crisis was over – they were releasing her at noon – they thought Rosalie ought to know.

She let him talk, hearing the exhaustion in his voice and knowing the fear and uncertainty that must have preceded it. He was a man who liked the familiar beyond all else; the trip had been her mother's idea, and until she got sick it would have been she who had managed everything. Coping alone in a bed-and-breakfast in a strange country would have made him irritable and anxious, and he'd have had no one to take it out on. He would have called Rosalie because he needed to talk to her, and not because her mother had told him to.

She imagined her mother lying pale in the hospital bed – frightened, too, by her own helplessness, knowing her husband's helplessness.

"Tell her we're all fine here," she said. "Tell her that Spenser and Victor are just fine. I've kept my eye on them." It was the only gift she could think of to send to her mother in that far-off hospital bed.

"I'll tell her. She'll be glad to hear it."

"Call me again in a day or two?"

"I will. We love you."

"You, too."

~

It became an obsession, then, with her, to get over and get that house in order. Even after the call from Versailles, when she heard her mother's voice sounding strong and happy and full of wonder at what she was seeing all around her, Rosalie felt she had betrayed her, let her down, by failing to take care of Spenser and Victor.

She phoned them the next Saturday morning and went over after lunch. She'd worn a summer skirt and sandals and a blouse, and carefully combed her hair – more cognizant now of the protocol. Spenser met her at the front door and, instead of taking her into the house, came down the front steps to lead her around to the back yard, giving her a tour of the flowerbeds as he went.

He became almost voluble as they moved from the front of the house to the back, identifying the perennials for her and explaining cultivation methods. They'd spent the morning dusting the rose bushes, he said.

In the back garden, Victor was seated in a lawn chair in the shade, beside a white wrought-iron table which held a large glass pitcher of iced tea and three glasses. He seemed moderately pleased to see her, and rose to his feet in greeting. His face had grown brown from sun, and he looked stronger and healthier than he had on her last visit.

The two of them escorted her around the yard, displaying the newly planted vegetable garden with its long straight strings to mark the rows, small stakes at each end with the seed packets tacked to them.

"We're trying a new variety of peas this year," Spenser said.

"Spenser ordered them from a catalogue, in January."

"But Victor insisted on some of our usual as well. You can see where we've marked them off."

Rosalie looked in bemusement at the order and the obvious hard work that made this garden. Not a thing was out of place, not a weed was visible. She recalled her mother coming home late on Saturdays in summer with brown paper bags full of carrots, peas and beans from the garden of these uncles.

"Do you dig the garden and cut the lawn yourselves?"

Spenser moved his head. "Not any more. We have someone come in to do the heavy work." He said it with regret.

They made their way back to the table in the shade, and Victor told her that they'd had two postcards from her mother. Only two weeks were left now before her parents would be back, and the brothers' confidence in their safe return seemed to have increased.

There was a plate of ice wafers on the table, pink and brown and pale yellow. Rosalie drank her tea, and listened to them discuss the possible whereabouts of the nest of a red-eyed vireo Victor had seen moving about the yard.

After a reasonable amount of time had elapsed, she stood and said, "Excuse me," and went up into the house.

It was dark and musty in there, and as she went up the back steps into the kitchen she saw with dismay the devastation that a month had accomplished. The kitchen was tidy enough, but it was also filthy. The floor was sticky as she walked across it, the counters layered in crumbs and grime. The kitchen table was covered with streaks and patches, globs and drips.

She sighed and went over to the stained sink, and picked up the dishcloth that was neatly hung over the tap. It retained its shape when she lifted it, and it reeked of staleness when she wet it. In a drawer she found a fresh one, and cleanser beneath the sink, and she began to scrub the counters. Through the dusty and water-splattered window she could keep an eye on the uncles: Victor was still seated, probably dropped off to sleep, and Spenser was wandering around the border of the vegetable garden.

As she worked, her irritation built. She'd need two full days at least to get this house cleaned up. She was angry with her mother for having established this routine, from which there was apparently no way out except for Rosalie to sneak around behind her uncles' backs, cleaning up their grime. Briefly she was angry with her grandmother, too, for not having insisted that these two men learn housework, but the thought made her immediately contrite. That was a different time, and there was a different set of rules. Her mother was the one to have arranged this better.

The counter and the tabletop clean, she again glanced out the window. Spenser was seated now as well, looking up at the house but apparently unable to see her, perhaps because of the angle of the sun. Were they participating in this charade? Were they waiting out there for her to finish with their domestic duties? And wasn't that what she'd wanted?

She rinsed the cloth and strode into the dining room. The table and sideboard were heavily coated with dust, clearly unused in all the time her mother had been away. And she would need a vacuum. She had no idea where the vacuum cleaner was, but she'd have to find it: she couldn't go out and ask them. That was not the way this game was played.

The vase of flowers, now dead and dry, was still in the centre of the table. She lifted it, the vase in one hand and the dishcloth in the other, and looked at the circle of clear shining wood where the base of the vase had been. It was like a mark that her mother had left for her, a glimpse of the way things ought to be. She stood there in her visiting clothes and closed her eyes.

The back screen door slammed and Spenser came up the stairs.

"We wondered if you were all right. We thought...." He had moved closer and he saw the cloth in her hand. His expression clouded. "We thought perhaps you'd left." He looked from the cloth up into her face.

"Don't do that," he said softly after a moment had passed. He put his hand out for the cloth, his long-fingered hand. "There's no need."

She handed him the cloth. "These flowers should be...."

"We can manage," he said more firmly.

"Why don't you get someone in, the way you do the garden? My mother could have arranged for someone...."

He was shaking his head. "We can't manage the garden any more. We can manage this. We always have."

You have not, she wanted to say. My mother has been the one who's managed.

But she nodded – annoyed with his obstinacy, but not enough

that she could tell him what a grimy mess his house was – and put the dead flowers back where they had been.

How did her mother do it? What was the elaborate ritual they'd worked out; what rules had she established to get through every week for all these years? Was it possible that they didn't even notice what she was doing, that the housework was so much a part of the women they knew – their mother and their sister – that they didn't even see it being done, or notice when it wasn't? It was the only explanation she could think of.

Their stubborn, impenetrable pride would not allow her an equal invisibility. Her mother had left this to her, without a word, not understanding that the ease of family does not necessarily pass from one generation to the next.

~

On the Thursday night she called to tell them that she'd been given tickets to the baseball game on Saturday afternoon, and said she was taking them to see it. Spenser insisted that they were fine, that they were busy with the garden, that they weren't that fond of baseball. But she was firm and determined, and for once his sense of what was polite and what was not worked in her favour.

The day was sunny and warm, with a mild breeze, when she picked them up at one. Both of them were wearing cardigans, and both of them wore straw hats. Spenser carried an umbrella. They had on soft white summer shoes and pale trousers. Spenser said that Victor had brought along his heart pills, just in case, and that he himself was carrying Aspirin in case the sun made any of their heads ache. The extent of their preparation unsettled her: she'd given far less thought to the outing itself than they had.

It took them several minutes of discussion before they concluded that Spenser would have to ride in the back seat, even if his legs were longer, because he bent more easily. Victor became worried that they'd left the door to the house unlocked and Rosalie had to go up and confirm that it was secure. At last they were set to go.

She'd never been to a professional baseball game before, but she had little time to attend to this one. She went back and forth to the refreshment kiosk several times, bringing them hot dogs and orange pop, and later cups of coffee. She went with them to find the restrooms on the pretext that she needed one for herself. When they came back, she insisted they move higher to get out of the sun. It was early in the season, and the stands were far from full.

Victor and Spenser seemed relaxed enough although not particularly engaged by the game. Victor kept nodding off and then jerking awake just as Rosalie began to fear he would tip over. She got up and moved past Spenser to sit down next to Victor, so that she could catch him if he did. After about half an hour of this, he seemed to have refreshed himself somewhat, and he sat more alertly, silently watching the players and the game.

Spenser seemed more determined to appear to be having a good time and occasionally he would lean across and say, "This is very nice," or "That was a good play." His heart didn't seem to be in it, but that didn't matter to Rosalie. She was doing this for her mother, not for them.

It took them a long time to walk back to the car. Victor had to pause several times to catch his breath. As they stood in the nearly deserted parking lot, waiting yet again to move closer to the car, Spenser told her not to be concerned: Victor would be fine again after he'd had a little rest.

In the car on the way home, Victor in the seat beside her asked, "Did you enjoy the game?"

"Yes," she said quickly, surprised that he would ask.

"You didn't seem to," he said.

She laughed. "It was a lovely afternoon."

When she reached their house, she parked at the curb, got out, and came around to help them. She helped Victor out first, and he stood on the sidewalk, leaning on his cane and watching as she reached in to help Spenser from the back.

"I can manage," he said sharply, and she nodded and stepped away. But then, as though to make amends, he handed her the umbrella. She took it and gripped it, fighting the urge to offer to help again as he slowly pulled himself out, and got himself upright.

The two men started up the walk, leaving her at the curb with thanks and assurances that they'd be fine. Near the house, Victor pointed at something in the flowerbed. Spenser stopped as well, turning to look and nodding, smiling a little down at Victor who was poking the soft soil with his cane. As she watched the two of them together, she felt the rootings of affection that her mother must have presumed would be there from the start.

She realized she was still holding Spenser's umbrella and she went up the walk to give it to him, and then startled each of them in turn with a brief peck on the cheek.

She looked up at the house. The windows shone and the whole place seemed to shimmer with its cleanliness. They were going to be offended, angry with her, when they opened their front door. She'd known this wasn't going to work from the moment she'd seen their straw hats and their cardigans earlier in the afternoon, and had felt her heart go soft. She gave them a small wave before she got in the car, and drove off.

They were reflected in her rearview mirror, still standing together on the sidewalk. It was too much to hope that they would understand why she had done it. Her only hope was that they might never notice that she had.

The Sign

The night when Rosamond's husband left was the night that followed the day when the butterflies lay with their wings spread flat along the ground. The children, not knowing that Joseph was about to go, lifted the butterflies by their wings and flung them into the air, but they drifted back down to settle on the pavement and the grass. The children tried not to step on them.

The night when Rosamond's husband left was the night before the day when the men in white noticed that Rosamond was living in the third floor suite. She'd been there six months by then, her fatness draped in bright scarlet and turquoise dresses that she washed in the men's room sink, her gold-plated jewellery ringing and clicking as she walked from floor to floor, urging her silent children from doorways and alcoves and out into the incessant sunlight. Her eyes were dark, and glittered.

Joseph was small and silent, and he went about his business – which was mending shoes – from early in the morning until long after the others in the building had slipped their money into small grey drawstring bags and gone to sit through the long bright evenings with their wives and families.

~

Joseph had come alone in March from the sunlit street to speak to the building supervisor about the space to let. The supervisor was a tall thin clothing designer who called himself Antonio and wore a gold ring through one ear. The men in white – a barber, a denturist and a chiropractor – saw Joseph pass their doors without looking in, and all of them saw the coolness on him despite the heat in the old building.

Antonio warned him about the light that poured in the window of the third floor suite, but Joseph pressed the deposit money into his slender hand. Antonio told him that the third floor suite was bad for business (he'd had it once himself): his customers would never find him there.

Joseph shook his head. "I have a sign," he said.

It was the only time the people in the building ever heard him speak.

The sign came on the morning of the following day. It was covered in flecks of silvered sequins, thousands of them that shimmered with the wind, and his name was on it, and his business, in strands of tiny coloured bulbs that formed the script, Joseph Fanon, Shoe Repair. The words were hard to read in all that sunlight, but no one who saw the sign could fail to imagine how it would look at night.

There were two men with Joseph in the cab of the pickup truck that brought the sign, and the men in white came out to watch where they would put it. For a long time, Joseph's companions stood in the back of the truck, while he stood on the sidewalk looking up at the brick face of the building. At last he nodded and the three of them went to work with ladders and screws and wires, and when they were finished the sign was immense above the door, as though the whole building were Joseph Fanon, Shoe Repair.

The men in white went in to phone their wives and after discussing it for a time, they did nothing. After all, their signs, small neatly lettered black on white beside the door, had not been hidden.

As soon as the sign was up, Joseph went upstairs to unpack the two trunks of shoes which had been under the sign in the back of the pickup. By the middle of the afternoon, the smells of leather and boot polish had reached the offices of the denturist, and he glanced up from the neat rows of headless teeth on his work bench to glimpse the scarlet hem of Rosamond, who was gliding past his door.

In time, the rich smell reached the street and the halls were full of people carrying shoes, following the smell past the chiropractor's office and up the stairs to the second floor where Antonio watched them, raw silk and scissors in his hands, and up again until they found the third floor suite where the scent was fullest. The procession grew, bearers of heel-less slippers and broken-soled shoes standing patiently in line, talking to one another about the things they'd read in newspapers and seen on television. The whole building buzzed with their quiet waiting-talk, and the air grew thick with the smells of waxes and creams.

And all the time the small children watched the people silently, listening, until Rosamond drifted through and sent them out into the sun.

The chiropractor saw that his own clients had to sidle past the line for Joseph Fanon, how sometimes they became entangled in it and took off one of their shoes to wait the wait and talk the talk and smell the smell. The chiropractor had to go out and remind his clients about their pinched nerves and their spinal realignments before they got too far into the building. Once they were past the designer's door on the second floor, they would not come out of the line no matter how he begged them.

He sent his wife up there one day, all the way to the top, for he could not go up there himself and leave his own business unattended. He nodded only briefly at her when she reached the place in line that passed his doorway. When she came back down much later she told him that Joseph Fanon had shaken his dark head at her evening shoe and handed it back to her. There was nothing, his expression had suggested, that could be done for it.

Others in line had told her that if you watched his hands while he was working, sometimes you didn't hear when people spoke to you, and Joseph had to push your mended shoe into your hands to wake you up. She wanted to try again with her day shoes, but the chiropractor shook his head and gave her a little money, and told her to go home.

Rosamond's children heard the men in white talking about the line of people, about Joseph, wondering if they should complain to the authorities about the sign. But the sunlit days went on and on, one after another, and the line continued to be there every morning after Rosamond had washed their feet in the men's room sink and put their shoes on and sent them out into the sun, and the authorities did not come.

In October, there was that day when the butterflies came down. Rosamond went to urge the children away from the line, the alcoves, and the doorways, and she found they were not there. She went out into the street and saw them stepping over fritillaries and admirals and tossing monarchs into the air.

Rosamond, in a dress of vermilion and turquoise, in silver slippers with straps across the arch, crossed into the square and lifted a mustard-white into her hands, bending so close that her earrings nearly touched its trembling antennae. She looked up into the empty trees and placed the butterfly on the grass again, and then she stepped carefully to the edge of the square where she stood for a long time, looking at Joseph's sign. Then she crossed the hot street and went back into the building.

In the morning, the butterflies were gone and so was Joseph Fanon. The men in white were pleased when the procession dwindled and the leather-polished smell began to dissipate, but they soon tired of going out into the hall to tell the people with the shoes that they needn't bother to climb the stairs because Joseph Fanon had gone.

The children were always in the hallways now. Rosamond no longer came to send them out because, although the sun still shone, the air in the streets had grown very cold since the day of the butterflies. When the men in white asked if their mother was in the third floor suite, the children nodded, and the barber and the chiropractor and the denturist climbed the stairs past the designer with wool and scissors in his hands, and they knocked on Rosamond's door.

She opened it and they saw the sun that poured in the window of the third floor suite and struck rows and rows of shoes against the opposite wall. With the light behind her, the men could see the outlines of Rosamond's fat thighs thorough the carmine and turquoise of her dress. They saw that her bare feet were firmly planted on the wood floor, far apart. She was holding her silver slippers in her hands.

"Your husband is gone," the barber said.

"He is looking for better shoes to fix."

"But people are still coming."

"He says their shoes are not worthy of his talent."

Rosamond's voice was even-toned and slow, so that her earrings barely moved when her words came out.

"Then the sign should be taken down," said the chiropractor.

"It's up to Joseph to take it down."

"Is he coming back?"

"He has always come back," she said. "He has always come back for the sign."

"And what about you? What about your children?" asked the denturist. "You have nothing here." They looked around the room. "No stove. No beds." They looked through her skirt at the outlines of her thick bare thighs. "You have no warm clothes, and winter has arrived."

"But I have shoes," she said, tossing her head at the opposite wall so that her long hair swung around her shoulders and her fat bare arms, and her jewellery jangled. "When we found Joseph, none of us had shoes. Now we have two hundred shoes."

She carried the silver slippers to the wall, and put them in the space on the top shelf.

The men in white went back down the stairs and told the building supervisor that the sign must be taken down so that the people (one went by just then and the barber had to go out in the hall and tell him that Joseph Fanon was gone) would stop coming. The dress designer said that as soon as he'd finished with the seam binding, he would take care of it.

The authorities came the next day, three people in blue uniforms: a policeman, a bylaw enforcement officer, and a social worker who shook her head at the silent children. The men in white stood at the foot of the stairs and watched the people in blue go out of sight at the second floor landing. They smiled at one another.

"The authorities will take care of it," they said.

When the dark began to come, early now that it was winter, the people in blue came back downstairs and walked past the offices of the men in white.

"Is it taken care of?" the barber called, snipping hair from the neck of the chiropractor.

"We told her the children would be taken away if she did not keep their feet clean," the social worker said, her voice echoing through the building.

"We told her we would take the sign down," called the bylaw enforcement officer, farther away, "and she'd have to pay the costs."

"We told her she'd be evicted," the policeman shouted, "if she didn't pay the rent."

When the men in white came out of the building, they saw that the policeman had put canvas bags on the heads of the parking meters in front of the building.

"They told me that if I got Joseph to mend their shoes," Rosamond called from the third floor window, her hair falling over her face and her breath turned blood red in the winter sunlight, "none of those things would happen."

~

It was soon after that when Rosamond began to dance. The denturist looked up from an improvement he was making to the second molar in his hand and saw her whirl past, jewellery flashing, bright fabric and dark hair spreading through the air around her as her bare feet moved down the hallway. She danced only a little that morning, her children watching wide-eyed and silent, and then she climbed the stairs to the third floor suite. But as the winter went on, she danced more often, longer, and swung her children around with her until they learned the way, and then all of them danced together or alone from the morning to the night.

"When will Joseph come?" the barber called as she whirled past.

"When he has found what he is looking for," she said into the door of the chiropractor and added to the denturist, breathing hard, "Then, he will need the sign."

With the lineups gone and winter here, there was no need to prod her children out into the sun and she whirled for the joy of all that leisure time, gold and red and blue and skin through the empty halls of the building. She spun with the children up and down the stairs, hugging them close to her, and their laughter clicked and shimmered like the sequins on the sign.

Rosamond, the men in white discovered as she swung past in

February and her skirt flew up to expose bare thighs, was dancing herself thin. The chiropractor looked over the back of the barber, to whose spine he was making an adjustment, and said to the denturist, "Now, no one comes. It was better with the lineups."

"How much longer can she dance? She'll have to stop eventually."

"When Joseph comes, he'll put a stop to it. He will make them put their shoes on."

"The children's feet are no longer clean. They're black, from all that dancing."

The barber said they should come in the middle of the night and take the sign down, in order to save their businesses.

"But if the sign is gone," the chiropractor said, "Joseph may not find her."

"And then what will she do?" the denturist said. "She has nothing but those shoes."

"The authorities will take care of them," the barber said. "That's what authorities are for."

~

They met at the church in the darkness, and even from that distance they could see that the light from the sign was shining up the sky. As they came closer they saw that the square was filled with people, hundreds of them in parkas and scarves and mittens, all of them looking toward the building. The huge sign sparked and glittered and shivered and shone, the coloured lights that said Joseph Fanon, Shoe Repair illuminating the thousands of shining sequins. And under it, on the pavement where the heat of the sign had melted the snow, Rosamond danced barefoot on the pavement.

She danced and danced until the men grew so tired from watching her that their eyes glazed over and they forgot why they were there. They watched her bright colours spin and twirl, and they watched her leap so high that she became a silhouette against the sign. When she was done, many hours later, there was a long silence and then she made two corners of her skirt and lifted them, and people from the square crossed over to drop money in the pouch that she had made.

~

For a while the men in white tried to keep busy with the dentures and the alignments and the haircuts of one another and one another's families, but there was no money in it. And so, instead of removing Joseph's sign, they took down their own and they went home to spend their remaining years with their wives and their grandchildren. This soon bored them and they found themselves sleeping late in the mornings to cut short the days, which left them wide-eyed as adolescents when midnight came.

They took to meeting in the square to watch the silent dance of Rosamond, to watch her slim bare thighs when her skirt flew up, and her black hair brush against her slender arms. Behind her in the building, Antonio cut through silk and wool and silk, silk with all manner of butterflies printed on it, and he watched her sleeping children, and in the morning while Rosamond slept he washed the children's feet in the men's room sink.

The winter came again and the men withdrew money from their banks to buy white goose-down parkas, and they dropped the change into Rosamond's skirt. They wished that their wives would dance.

One night in February, when the dance was ended and the people had all gone except the men in white, when Rosamond was putting her money into a grey canvas drawstring bag, a pickup truck with three men in it pulled up to the hooded parking meters.

Joseph Fanon got out and looked at the sign and glanced at Rosamond. But he didn't know her thin, and he went past her into the building and up the stairs and the men in white saw the light in the third floor suite come on. Joseph lifted the rows and rows of shoes, and packed them out of sight, even the silver slippers. At last the light went out.

Joseph came back down and nodded at his men, who began to take down the sign with ladders and wire clippers and screwdrivers. Afterward they went and got the trunks of shoes from the third floor suite, and they put them in the truck.

Rosamond stood in the shadow where the light had been and watched them work. They loaded the ladders and the big dark sign into the back of the pickup truck, their breaths white as ice and coming fast from the effort. And then they drove away.

When all sound was gone, the men in white watched Rosamond. She took a step, and then another, spinning and twisting until she lifted herself right off the ground. The doors of the building opened, and Rosamond spun laughing down into the street, and gathered her children into the air with her.

The men sighed and lay back in the snow, too tired to find their black and white signs and put them up again.

Rosamond ran into the square and danced over the men in white. She danced barefoot across the snow, her feet never quite touching ground, and disappeared into the darkness of the trees – her children dipping and fluttering like butterflies behind her.

The Hilltop

"Maybe he shouldn't be here while I'm gone," Alex said, one thick hand on his belly. "Neighbours might get the wrong impression."

Hester shrugged softly and leaned into the circle of yellow light, wiping away the last ring of coffee from the plastic tablecloth.

"Then again…" Alex studied her, his leg slung over the arm of his chair, "…might look strange if we farmed him out."

She watched her hands. They folded the dishrag into a square and pressed it between their palms.

"Who'd we farm him out to?" she said, making it more a statement than a question. She knew better than to say anything else. Part of what she knew about Alex, which was entirely too much of late, was his tendency to change his mind at the very last instant if he felt he was being pushed. He got pleasure from doing that, from proving his control.

The back door slammed, and both of them looked toward the sound of Jay, stamping the snow from his boots.

"Got it started," he called, unnecessarily loud. Even after two weeks he was still not used to so small a house. "You ready to go?"

"Bus doesn't leave till eleven," Alex said, leaning forward a little so he could see Jay in the kitchen. "Still time for a beer."

Hester put down the dishrag on the tablecloth and crooked an index finger through the elastic band that held her long brown hair away from her face, pulling the elastic down until it came free. She smoothed her hair back, twisted the band around it, and slipped past Alex on her way to hang the dishrag over the kitchen tap.

This morning, she'd plucked another grey hair from along the line of her scalp. The grey ones were of a different texture, breakable. Pulling them reminded her of culling dead flowers in the middle of summer: she wouldn't be forty for another year.

"You want one?" Jay asked quietly as he bent for the beer, his red-jacketed shoulders silhouetted by the refrigerator light. When he turned, a can of Pilsner in each hand, his face was red from the cold. The kitchen smelled of him, fresh and clean from the winter night.

She shook her head. "I've got to be at work at twelve."

"You can drop Hester at the Hilltop," Alex said from the living room, "after you drop me at the bus. Jessie Olchowy will drive her home."

Jay snapped one beer open with his thumb and sucked at foam, his grey eyes on Hester over the top of the can, his back to Alex.

"No problem," he called, but he didn't take his eyes from Hester. Instead, he let them move from her face, let them skim her breasts – she could almost feel the touch – then move back up to meet her eyes again. Something in her throat could too easily have turned into a sound, and she looked away.

She watched Jay's feet, white-socked, his legs, as he went into the living room.

"You got to be nuts," he said to Alex, handing him a Pilsner. "Drinking beer when it's this cold out. Must be minus thirty."

"Colder 'n that," Alex answered firmly. "You can tell by the frost on the inside of the door. It'll be a real son-of-a-bitch tonight. Always is, when it's clear like this."

Jay almost smiled. "You're bad as Dad when he quit smoking. Proud of the pain. Worse it got, better he liked it."

Hester leaned, her arms crossed, against the counter in the darkened kitchen, and watched them talk. Jay was so much more cautious with Alex than he'd been at first. But Alex didn't seem to notice. Too busy playing the big brother.

They weren't actually related. Jay's parents had burned up in a house fire and Jay was taken in by Alex's family when he was three. Alex had been fourteen when Jay came to live with them, and he always said that Jay had worshipped the ground he walked on from the moment he arrived. Hester didn't believe that until Jay got here, and she saw the admiration in his eyes and heard it in his voice. At first he didn't mind the weather, didn't mind the prairie. He was just happy to be here with Alex.

Alex was shorter and darker than Jay, and a little softer. He complained that he was getting old and flabby, but his lack of tone was a triumph, too, proof that he no longer made his living from physical labour. What he and Jay had in common was a certain fierceness bred on the tobacco farm down east. Neither of them ever wanted to work for Alex's father again – the spectre of doing so had driven Alex to several unlikely jobs, as it would probably Jay as well. But their conversation always returned to him, to the lean, hard man who'd raised them.

The newness of Jay, so close, revealed the familiarity of Alex. It was as though Hester hadn't really looked at him in years. Now she saw his leg slung over the arm of the chair, his thick hand around a beer can atop his knee. And she saw Jay's even muscle through his jeans, the hardness of his calves and thighs.

In the darkness of the kitchen, she closed her hands into soft fists against her ribs.

~

Alex was going to Edmonton to pick up the hearse from the car repair and to order caskets and outer boxes and some other things he needed. He would do his business tomorrow and, weather permitting, be back in Barwell Thursday noon. Hester sat in the back seat of the Chev and listened to him give instructions on what to do if someone died while he was out of town. He was making fun of Jay.

"And then you just sort of ease their eyes shut…."

"Oh, God," Jay said, his bare fingertips going white on the seat-back as they edged around a corner. Hester wanted to put her gloved hand out to touch his arm, to remind him Alex was teasing.

"Most of the time they drop dead in the middle of the night," said Alex, as he slowed the car into the white cloud of exhaust from the Greyhound, which was unloading in front of the Barwell Hotel. "They're real inconsiderate that way." He laughed.

In the dark of the back seat, Hester closed her eyes. Why did he say such things?

Alex slugged Jay on the shoulder to say goodbye to him, and Hester climbed out to kiss Alex as Jay slid over to the driver's seat.

"Be good," Alex said when the two of them were standing on the sidewalk.

"I will," she said. "I love you."

"You, too," he answered, finishing their litany. Their breaths, iced, filled the space between them.

She watched as he handed his suitcase to the driver and climbed up on the bus before she got back into the car. She sat close to the window. Jay stretched his right arm across the seat and looked back, ready to reverse.

"Wait," she said quietly. "Not yet. Not until the bus is gone."

Jay glanced at her, and shifted back to neutral. After a moment he said, "Never figured Alex for an undertaker."

"Him either." She smiled. "Thought he was getting into furniture."

"I couldn't stand it."

"Alex is good at it." She wondered if saying that made it sound like she was putting Alex down. Or Jay.

After several minutes, the bus rolled away through the snow, Alex still on it, and Jay edged into the icy wake. Now she could think of nothing to say. She was embarrassed by the growing silence, made more obvious by the grind of tires on snow, by the sound of the reluctant engine. She was afraid that Jay might start to whistle, or to tap his fingers on the wheel.

They'd never run short of things to talk about before. While Alex had been at work, they'd drifted into conversations that had gone on for hours at a time. It wasn't the kind of talk she had with the truckers at the Hilltop. That kind skipped and danced at best. With Jay, talk plunged deep and stayed there, but there was something playful to it, too, something that kept them both at it, looking for more talk and more, for subjects to try out on one another. Politics, religion: they'd covered a lot of territory. They didn't always agree, but they'd never run out of things to say.

Until now, as he edged the car along the frozen road, and she could think of nothing. Not a word that could possibly be appropriate. Yesterday afternoon he had kissed her, and she had kissed him back, and they'd found themselves pressed so close against each other that they could not possibly have left anything unfinished if they'd had a half hour of certain privacy. But yesterday there'd been no certainty of privacy and they had drawn apart. They'd avoided one another since.

"You missed the turn," she said suddenly.

He slammed on the brakes. The back end of the car swung out and the vehicle began to spin, to spin them slowly over the smooth ice until at last they came to rest near the edge of the ditch.

Hester laughed suddenly, her heart pounding from the spin. Jay laughed too, less certainly.

"You okay?"

"Of course."

She swallowed.

"Alex warned me not to brake on this stuff but it takes some getting used to." He reached out and took her hand. She moved across the seat toward him. He said, "Why don't they put down sand, or salt?"

The road was empty and unlit, and he pressed his face into her woollen hat. He touched her cheek and her forehead with his lips.

"When it gets this cold," she said, "the sand slides off the ice just like everything else." Her voice sounded thin.

"Salt too?"

"You'd need too much of it."

"He's gone," he said softly into her hair.

She closed her eyes and nodded. The feel of Jay so near was powerful, his smell so clean. She wanted to climb inside that smell, to feel it all around her.

"I wish you didn't have to go to work."

She touched his face, and he took her hand in his. He slipped two fingers inside her glove and rubbed the bare palm of her hand. "I hate winter clothes," he said. "I hate this cold." He looked toward the window. "I have to get out of here." After a moment he put his forehead against hers and closed his eyes.

"Where to?" she asked, her lips against his cheek.

He shrugged. "Vancouver, maybe. Somewhere."

"Not back where you came from. And not here. Anyplace will do."

"Yeah." He moved his head away and looked at her. "He thinks it's so different from the farm, but it's not. It's just the same. Tiny community, no future. Every day the same. I don't know how you stand it."

She felt apologetic for the place, its winter. She knew what he was talking about, remembered a time when she'd wanted to get away more than anything in the world. She didn't remember when that urge had faded, but she knew that it was gone.

"I grew up here. Maybe it looks different when you're born to it." She looked out the ice-fogged windows at the frozen night. "It looks different in the summer. I guess we wait for that."

"I don't want to wait."

He leaned down and kissed her and she kissed him back and then, barely knowing she was about to speak, she said, "He's my husband, Jay. And he might as well be your brother."

"That's another reason why I gotta go."

She didn't need to have said it: it hadn't changed a thing. She moved across the seat toward the window.

He put the car in gear. After he'd backed up across the road to turn the car around, they started toward the turnoff that he'd missed.

"When you get home tomorrow morning," he said after a moment, "I'm going to be there. And you're going to be there." He looked over at her. "No one else. Just us."

~

The coffee shop was attached to a service station on the edge of the highway about three kilometres out of Barwell, in the middle of an expanse of prairie. It had been named the Hilltop as a joke: from its windows you could see for miles in every direction.

The Hilltop was busy. It always was on winter nights this cold. Truckers scattering shivers of crystal along the highway couldn't resist the lights and chrome and coffee.

As Hester was hanging up her coat in the back, she asked Jessie Olchowy for a ride home after work.

"Alex's brother's got the car."

"Sure thing," said Jessie. "Any time. You know that." Tying her apron around her wide middle, she nodded toward the kitchen. "Gonna be a son of a bitch tonight."

Same words Alex had used, Hester remembered. "You can handle it," she said.

"Damned rights. That's not the point. I'm getting too old to be slinging burgers and eggs around a kitchen all night long."

Hester smiled as she walked away, pinning the orange headband with the little Hilltop peak firmly to her hair. She liked Jessie who, at the age of fifty-one – a short, greying strawberry blonde – was about forty pounds overweight and didn't seem to give a damn. But Jessie traced scandal like a magpie after road kill, and Hester was glad it was so busy that there'd be no time for talk.

She'd once planned to work at the Hilltop only until children came along, and the fact that none had, or would, had been not a sudden awareness but an increasing realization, and as a result it had never forced her into a choice about what she would do next. It was quite possible that she wouldn't do anything next but this. Sometimes it seemed to her that her entire life was just going to gradually come unrolled like an old bandage, without even a decent wound at the centre to recommend it.

Normally she didn't mind the work: it gave her an opportunity to talk to people who knew what was going on outside. Truckers passed through from all over North America, and she liked to guess where they came from by their accents and their slang. But tonight she didn't feel like talking. The work seemed tedious and unending, the time to pass with excruciating slowness. She tried to keep her mind off Jay, off Alex, but it did no good. As she wiped tables clean and put out cutlery and glasses, she'd see Alex and Jay together, Alex in the front seat of their car, Alex kissing her goodbye – and then suddenly and unexpectedly she'd be kneed by her longing for Jay.

~

The only person that Alex had ever lost, who really meant something to him, was his mother. He'd never talked about her illness or her death, but he used to talk about the funeral all the time, going over and over the details until Hester couldn't understand why he never sounded bored when he started in on it again. He didn't talk about it any more, now that he was in the business himself.

It was things like that that irritated her, when he'd repeat stories to her a dozen times as though she didn't mean anything, as though she were a cardboard audience and he was trying out an act. Sometimes when she'd watch him undressing she'd thought: his is the only body I'm ever going to know. And she'd resented him for that.

Two men who ought to have memorized the menu after the number of times they'd been in here dawdled over their selections and asked for her advice. She warned herself to be careful how she acted, reminded herself to pay attention to what she was doing, but it was like prodding a reluctant goat. Her mind wanted to go someplace else, to stretch out next to Jay's.

~

Jessie always looked about five years older than she was at the end of a busy night. It was most obvious in summer when the day was on them when they came off the shift. Usually Hester was tired, too, but this morning she felt strong and wide awake.

As they sat in the Cutlass, waiting for the engine to warm and the windows to clear, Jessie put her head back and closed her eyes. Hester was anxious to be off, wanted to scrape the windows clear and go, but she held herself still.

"I'm going to quit," Jessie said, her eyes still closed.

"You'll feel better if you get some sleep," Hester said.

Jessie moved her head slowly back and forth. "No. I really mean it this time."

Hester pushed her irritation down. She turned toward Jessie and said firmly, "Anyone would be tired, doing what you do. Looking after Dave, Ellen's kids half the time. Working all night long." She put her hand out and touched the arm of Jessie's coat. "All that would wear anyone out."

Jessie took Hester's hand. "You oughta quit, too," she said. "Do something with your life. If you don't, in ten years you'll be me."

Hester laughed and said, "That wouldn't be so bad." It didn't sound very convincing, but she didn't know how to fix that. "You want me to drive?" she asked.

"I'll do it," Jessie said. She sighed and put the car in gear.

~

As they crept slowly over the ice of the back roads, Hester talked about Alex's trip to Edmonton and the things they had to do when he got back. She hoped that Jay would have the sense not to be waiting up with all the lights on. She had her eyes so closely on the spot in the distance where her house would appear that she almost missed the Chevrolet in the left-hand ditch. When they were nearly past it, she put her gloved hand on Jessie's shoulder, and pointed.

"That's my car."

Jessie edged over to the shoulder and stopped. Just behind them, the blue Chev was nosed down in the snow, dark and silent, its windows ice-fogged.

"Alex's brother is in there. He dropped me off at work."

"He probably hitched a ride."

"Who would come down this road in the middle of the night?" Hester asked, too sharply. She was afraid that she would never be able to move.

Jessie said, "You want me to look?"

And then they were both outside, Hester skidding down the

embankment with Jessie right behind her. She opened the driver's door.

"He's not in here," she said, her voice thickening with fear.

Already she was hunting around the car for tracks, looking toward the field where he would be frozen white to death....

"Jay!" she screamed across the silent, frozen spread of prairie. "Jay!"

"He's here," Jessie said quietly behind her and Hester spun toward her, toward the car. "He's in the back."

And he was, all but his face covered in the heavy green army blanket which usually served as a seat cover. He looked cold, but almost calm.

He said, "I thought you'd never get here."

Hester felt relief for only a moment before she wanted to hit him, hard, across the face. "You idiot," she said. "You could have died."

"Don't be ridiculous," he said.

"I'm not." She took a breath. "You scared the hell out of me."

Jessie was watching them, curious. Hester reached into the car for Jay, and Jessie took one arm. Together, they helped him up the bank across the road and into Jessie's warm back seat. Hester climbed in beside him and turned on the interior light to study his face. The tips of his ears and nose were bitterly red, but there seemed to be no frostbite.

"You could have frozen to death," she whispered.

"No way."

Jessie got into the driver's seat and slammed her door.

"Of course you could."

"Only ran out of gas an hour ago."

Hester turned her head so that Jessie could not see her expression in the rear view mirror. She wanted to shake him, to shake some sense into him.

"What happened, kid?" Jessie asked from the driver's seat.

"Braked for a rabbit. A jackrabbit. White." He laughed. "I missed it."

Jessie had been revived by the event and as she drove them back to the house she cheerfully related tales of acquaintances and strangers who'd frozen pieces of their bodies in Alberta winters. One man from a town nearby had frozen all of his, and hadn't been found until spring.

Jay was appreciative of her stories, but still did not seem to relate them to what he'd just been through.

"He didn't look so good," Jessie was saying to Jay over her shoulder. "As you can well imagine. But you'll be fine. Young people recover fast."

Hester felt Jay's leg, trembling a little as it began to warm, against hers.

There was no doubt why she wanted him. He was her last chance motel, her final kick at the cat. The question was why he wanted her. Was it a remnant of his awe for Alex, the last shred of his wanting to have what Alex had? Maybe it was less than that. Maybe it was just that she was here.

Jessie was right: young people recovered fast. They thought they'd live forever. One incident, one moment, one brush against significance, didn't matter when you had all that time. Jessie would remember this night, its detail, far longer than Jay would. Hester would remember, too.

"You want me to come in, help get him settled?" Jessie asked as they turned into the driveway.

Jay looked at Hester, widening his eyes.

"No, thanks, Jessie," Hester said. "I'll manage."

After she'd helped Jay out, Hester leaned her head into the car.

"Thanks for the ride," she said.

"Okay," Jessie said, her arm hooked over the back of the front seat.

"See you tonight?"

Jessie sighed. "Oh, probably. We carry on, don't we?"

"Yeah," Hester said. "We do."

She straightened and slammed the door shut. As the car moved down the driveway away from her, she paused for a moment, looking at the frozen landscape, knife-edged against the blackness of the sky.

Travelling by Mexico

Ten or twelve days later, when the ship had already left without her and she was sitting in a hotel in Acapulco, Kate realized that it was only after Carla had left that she'd taken any real notice of Robert.

As Kate had not yet found the courage to venture out of the hotel, she had a lot of time to think, and after a while the sequence offered up a kind of logic. It was so unusual for anything she did to make sense, or at least for her to recognize the sense of what she did, that she wrote this particular illumination down on a little piece of paper which she put in a pocket of her handbag. Months later, back at home, she found she could take this paper out and read it, and still feel surprised at the insight.

It wasn't anything that changed her life. But it did matter. It was something.

It was the woman's eagerness as she came on board which attracted Kate's attention, its stark contrast to the worried, casual, and even bored expressions on the faces of so many of the passengers. Kate also noticed the incongruity of her long-sleeved scarlet dress and wide-brimmed scarlet hat against her white socks and tennis shoes, but mostly it was the enthusiasm the woman made no attempt to hide.

Almost springing with each step, she strode past the indifferent welcomes of the men in tuxedos and white gloves who were directing passengers to their cabins. As Kate watched, she stepped around suitcases and excused her way through groups of milling people, her dark eyes bright and taking in everything – including, briefly, Kate.

Kate had arrived an hour before, and had already seen her cabin and just about everything else on board. She thought how much better off she'd be if she could summon some of that eagerness herself. Unfortunately, it wasn't the kind of thing you could fake.

A man who was a good deal older followed the woman, weighed down by two matching suitcases: one chestnut, one dust green. He kept his eyes on her slender back, and he looked both indulgent and pleased. He was wearing one of those caps certain men wear when they board ships, white with a black brim, an anchor embroidered on the front. His beard and his hair were grey and neatly trimmed, but no one would mistake him for the woman's father.

After a few moments, she disappeared from Kate's view, and then the man did, too.

Kate went to the upper deck, where she ordered a beer from a waiter and went to the rail to await the ship's departure. On the dock below her, dark-skinned, dark-haired men in sequined turquoise suits and sombreros with black pompons blew on trumpets and strummed guitars and violins. They looked out of place in the cool Los Angeles winter evening, the grey shipyards behind them. Their trumpets were too loud.

Farther off, a group of blond, tanned and muscular young men and women joked with one another as they stood with scissors at intervals along a net filled with balloons. The decks had become crowded with people holding drinks as the scheduled time of departure approached, occurred, then passed. Most of the passengers seemed to be travelling in pairs or foursomes. There were older women with other older women, but most of the pairs consisted of one from each of the two genders. Like to the ark, Kate thought.

She alternately wished that Will's family could see this, and was grateful that they couldn't. Thanks to *The Love Boat*, they imagined that it was solitary people, spiritually if not physically, who came up the gangplanks of cruise ships, and that the main function of such trips was to give everyone time to get into pairs before they disembarked.

The woman in scarlet appeared almost directly below Kate. Her long dark hair was hatless now, and she pressed through the crowd which was two or three deep until she reached the rail. She turned and put her arm out, taking the man's hand and drawing him up beside her. She pointed at the band and pointed at the docks, chattering, oblivious to the looks she was getting from the people she'd edged aside. She kept glancing at her watch and looking up at the bridge expectantly. The man still wore his cap, and Kate couldn't see his face.

About ten minutes after their scheduled departure time, the ship began to edge away from the dock. "La Cucaracha" rose into the cool night air (Kate could hardly believe her ears), but was drowned for a moment by one blast from the ship's horn. The woman laughed and pointed as the balloons, released, floated back toward Los Angeles. The man leaned down and kissed the woman lightly on the head, and she threw her arms around him and kissed him back.

A lot of people cheered.

~

There was a bowl of fruit in Kate's cabin and a bottle of champagne with two glasses. She put these on the empty bed across from the one she'd chosen for herself, and looked at them occasionally as she dressed for dinner. A little white card said, "To Kate and Eleanor. Bon voyage." These things were from the travel agent who, by wording the card the way he did, had managed to extricate himself from the dismay Kate felt toward everyone else connected with her being on this cruise.

The trip had been a Christmas present from Will's parents. It was more generous and more complicated than just a Christmas present: it had been a gesture, a way of saying that a year was long enough. If she met someone else, the ticket said, they would learn to live with it.

In order to maintain the balance they'd always been so careful about before Will died, they'd also given a ticket to Eleanor, Kate's sister-in-law. Eleanor wasn't supposed to meet someone else. Her husband was still alive. She was only supposed to be company for Kate, maybe to give her a shove when necessary, make sure she got busy and enjoyed herself. At least, that's how it had seemed at Christmas.

Two days before they left, Eleanor had come down with some unspecified ailment which made her throw up all the time. When Kate's suitcases were already packed and her taxi ordered, Eleanor had decided that she couldn't possibly travel, given the way she felt. Especially not to Mexico.

On the way to the airport it had occurred to Kate that her travelling alone could quite easily have been the plan from the beginning. She almost told the driver to turn his car around, but after thinking for a while about the proportion of her in-laws' disappointment, she said nothing.

~

When Kate arrived at her assigned place in the dining room, the woman she'd seen on deck was seated at the same table – along with her companion, and two elderly couples who identified themselves as the Murrays and the Munroes. The woman's name was Carla. Kate could not later recall if her last name was ever mentioned.

"And I am Robert Dirkson," the man said. He was wearing glasses and peering over the menu, and he looked even greyer without his cap. Kate wondered what Carla saw in him.

When Carla discovered that Kate had a return ticket – it turned out that none of the others at the table did – she said she was green with envy. She'd never been on a cruise before, she said, and she went on to point out some of the details that enthralled her – which was nearly everything: the chandeliers, the elaborate menu, the waiters in their tuxedos. "Look at that!" she kept saying, interrupting herself. She couldn't wait to get to Mexico, she said, and visit all those cities.

Kate had noticed that the hem on their waiter's jacket was held up with safety pins. After listening to Carla for a while, she regretted the observation. It may have been the wine that Mr. Murray poured her, but she suddenly wished everything to be perfect. She wished she'd ordered something more interesting than chicken.

Carla had done some research in preparation for the cruise. Acapulco, she informed them, had been a busy port for nearly five hundred years. Galleons entering the bay, filled with silks and spices, silver and gold from the Philippines and China, were popular targets for pirates, and the seabeds were littered with treasure. The residents had built fortifications near the mouth of the bay, but most of these were destroyed – along with the city itself – in a late-eighteenth-century earthquake.

Carla was an artist – an amateur, she assured them. She'd brought her watercolours with her, and three cameras, and twenty rolls of film. She sounded as though she planned to get all of Mexico down on paper of one sort or another and take it home with her.

But as Carla spoke, their southern destination took on colour in Kate's mind. Blue seas glittered like booty, stone forts sank in clouds of grey dust, and for the first time she felt anticipation.

Carla was wearing a flowered wrap-around dress which showed off her breasts and her narrow waist. Her hair and eyes were dark, her mouth small and expressive. Kate guessed her to be about twenty-five, whereas the man who was with her, Robert, was closer to Kate's age. Forty-five. Maybe even fifty. Kate tried to remember being twenty-five herself, and remembered it was when she had married Will.

Carla's enthusiasm and the wine seemed to bring the Murrays and the Munroes gradually to life, and conversation moved around the table, onto other subjects. Mrs. Murray confessed her tendency to seasickness and warned them of the enormous cost of medical attention on a cruise. They'd travelled on ships many times before.

Mrs. Munroe remarked that she hoped their late departure wasn't an indication of inefficiencies to come. Something crossed Carla's face as she agreed with this. She said, with an affectionate look at him, that Robert was more accepting of delays than she. She said he taught history at a college in Seattle. The way she said it, it was intended to explain a lot.

The main course was served. Kate looked around at the others' plates and decided she should have ordered the sea bass rather than the chicken. Or maybe the shrimp and linguini – Carla had ordered that, and the way her face went when she took the first bite confirmed that it was delicious.

Mrs. Murray indicated the empty seat between Kate and Mr. Munroe, and asked if Kate's husband were unwell.

"My sister-in-law was going to come with me," Kate said. "She was taken ill at the last moment."

"You're travelling alone?" said Mrs. Munroe whose hair had a bluish tinge. "What a shame."

"But so much better than not travelling at all," said Carla. She smiled encouragement at Kate. "I think that's great, that you came anyway."

Kate smiled back, feeling fraudulent.

"But what about your husband?" Mrs. Murray insisted, moving her glance to Kate's face from the rings on her left hand.

"Now, Ellie..." her husband started.

"I'm a widow," Kate said quickly. It would need to be said at some point. She might as well get it done.

"Now, that's sad," Carla said, and looked at Robert.

Robert told Kate he was sorry, as though saying it on behalf of the two of them. He said it evenly, without pity.

"Oh, it's all right," Kate said brightly. She'd intended to mean that they shouldn't let it put a damper on their evening. But the brightness didn't sound appropriate. Embarrassed, she looked away.

~

The following afternoon, Kate noticed Carla several times, walking the decks outside. She was bundled in jackets and scarves and wearing a woollen hat. There was no sign of Robert.

"I've discovered I don't like ships too much," Carla had announced evenly at noon. "They're confining. I've been up since six, and I ran out of things to do at seven." She looked around her for support.

Kate nodded, mainly because no one else did.

"It's a holiday," Robert said. "You have to get used to the pace."

"How can I get used to the pace?" she said, looking at him incredulously. "Everyone has a rhythm, and mine's faster than the ship's. I can't get used to it."

He shrugged. "You could play blackjack. Shoot traps."

Carla looked at Kate. "I can't wait till we land, can you? Get out there in Mexico and go somewhere. Do things."

They'd had so much wine at lunch that Kate needed to lie down. She spent the rest of the afternoon reading a mystery she'd found in the ship's library, moving from one deck to another, trying to get her sea legs. She went outside once, but found it too cold and grey and windy to want to stay there. The clouds had lifted briefly as they moved through the Cedros Islands just past noon, but they'd returned soon after to grey the sky and the sea. There was no longer any sign of land.

Kate felt the ship was moving with determination toward Mexico, but Carla was irritated when she came to dinner. She was tense and quiet, alternately picking at her manicured nails and toying with her food. Tonight Kate had ordered the halibut, and was longing for Mr. Murray's steak.

Mrs. Murray, feeling unwell, had left right after the soup to go to bed. Kate thought of asking Mr. Murray why they kept going on cruises if it made Mrs. Murray sick, but didn't.

The Munroes had had too many pre-dinner drinks and were so busy talking about their family in Newport that they seemed unaware of Carla's distraction.

As their plates were being removed Carla said abruptly, "To think it's another whole day and a half before we can get off."

"You're not ill, too, are you?" Mrs. Munroe beside her asked, focussing carefully.

"No. I'm bored. Bored stiff. Bored half to death." She raised her neat eyebrows. "Aren't you?"

"Bored?" said Mrs. Munroe, amazed. "How could anyone be bored? There's never enough time...."

"She's young," Mr. Munroe said gently. "Probably doesn't play bingo." He winked at Kate.

Mrs. Munroe narrowed her eyes at him.

Kate suddenly remembered a tent in a three-day rain somewhere near Jasper, two or three summers ago, Will refusing to give up and go home. It was his holiday, he said.

Carla looked down at her plate. "I'm also stuffed. All we ever do is eat."

"Stiff and stuffed," Robert said, smiling. "Have a glass of wine. Enjoy yourself."

"I've done some calculations," Carla said to Kate. "We're going to be on this ship for more than seventy-five percent of this trip."

Kate smiled, but felt her spirits sink.

"Four and a half days out of seven. Can you believe it? Not to mention all the nights."

"What do you think 'cruise' means?" asked Robert mildly.

Carla left the table before dessert. She had to get outside, she said. She couldn't stand to look at all that food. She said it was disgusting. Robert watched her go.

Kate remembered wondering what Will would have done if she had screamed. She hadn't done it, of course. She'd just thought about it, over and over again, while they sat in the tent in the rain, playing cards, reading, even making love to kill time. What she'd really wanted to do was leave, but instead she'd imagined herself screaming. At the top of her lungs, from the bottom of her throat.

Neither Carla nor Robert appeared for breakfast or lunch the following day. Kate didn't see them anywhere on board, although she found herself looking for them. She wandered around and around the ship, trying to walk off her meals. An aerobics class in one of the lounges had been overcome by what seemed to Kate an affected hilarity. She felt no temptation to join them.

The air was growing warmer, and a pale cuff of land appeared on the eastern horizon late in the afternoon. Kate sat at a table outside and wrote a thank-you letter to Will's parents, telling them how good the food was and how many activities there were on board.

She also wrote a get-well note to Eleanor that might have been sarcastic or might have been sincere, depending on how you read it.

The wedge of land grew wider and higher as she completed the second letter. The air was now noticeably warm – men and women had come to sit in deck chairs in their bathing suits – and the sun behind them lit a treeless, empty land. The Baja Peninsula. She could see buildings on the shore, pale adobe reddened by the sun. She watched at the rail, wind tangling her hair, as the buildings grew closer together.

The ship rounded a point of land and a town at last came into view. Kate thought how pleased Carla would be to see it. The captain began to talk over the loud speaker but the wind blew his words away.

~

There was no scheduled shore excursion at Cabos san Lucas and yet the ship and the buildings had stopped moving past one another. Far below, a launch emerged from the shadow of the Duchess and began to bounce across the waves toward the shore. There were three people in the tender, some boxes, one dust-green suitcase. Carla was in the middle, her hand holding her hair at the nape of her neck to keep it from blowing around.

Standing at the rail, Kate thought of their dinner table, of the Munroes and the Murrays. She thought of all the days ahead and she wanted to shout, to hail out over the wind and water, to call Carla back again.

~

Before they'd even left L.A., Kate had signed up for city tours in every port they'd put into down the coast: Mazatlan, Puerto

Vallarta, Ixtapa, Acapulco. As the battered tour bus left the parking lot for Mazatlan, Kate noticed Robert come off a shuttle wagon and board the bus behind hers. He'd told them at dinner the night before that his wife had been taken ill. No one had asked why he hadn't gone ashore with her. The dinner had been quiet, purposeful. The Munroes didn't order wine, and Kate found herself able to resist dessert.

She'd felt tired when she woke up and she'd had to force herself to take the tour. Now she was relieved to be inside the bus. She'd been surprised and disturbed by the insistent hawkers who'd been waiting for them outside the harbour compound.

"Lady, you buy. Lady."

The bus lurched forward and as the driver began his patter, she looked down from the windows and into the small dark homes they passed. Shards of glass like knives stood within her reach, embedded in the tops of concrete walls. Dead chickens hung in store windows.

She was the only person on the bus who was travelling alone. Being surrounded by so many couples all the time made her think of Will, just as she was beginning to be able not to. Her singleness was too obvious on this trip, but the thought that finding a partner might be expected of her made her feel even more displaced. She wished she were invisible.

If she'd chosen and paid for this trip herself, she'd be entitled to have a lousy time. But she hadn't. Every unfamiliar sight reminded her of that, by reminding her of her obligation to record it for those who had paid her way.

At a yellow-gold church, women sat on the steps with small brown children in their laps, their thin arms up, hands out. Kate avoided looking in their eyes. Inside the church, she felt awkward, sight-seeing where there were people who needed to pray. But when the tour was hurried out before she'd had a chance to look at even half the carvings, she felt a Carla-like irritation at being herded.

Their final stop was a shopping plaza, where they were given beer in the warm sun when they got off the bus. This was what the tour had been aimed at: getting tourist dollars into local shops. Now, there was no rush to get the passengers moving, and other buses accumulated behind them.

She noticed Robert pondering jewellery as she wandered through the plaza, and a few minutes later he was at her side.

"She wasn't really sick," he said.

"She was stir crazy. So am I."

He nodded, looking down at her empty bottle. "Can I get you another beer?"

"I don't think so. No." She looked down at her bottle, too. The beer made her feel dizzy in the heat, but no more amenable to shopping. "Why didn't you go with her?"

"She didn't want me to." He smiled. "She was escaping."

Kate nodded.

"Besides," he said, shrugging, "I wanted to go on this cruise. Why should I change my plans?"

~

"It's the fifth time she's left me," he said later, back on board. "So far, the most expensive." He gave a little laugh but Kate could hear no bitterness in it, nor had there been any in his words.

They were standing at the rail as the ship moved them on again, away from Mazatlan. The sun was sinking red, and Kate enjoyed the feeling of the warm night, like summer back home. It was nice to have someone to stand with. Made her feel less at sea.

She smiled.

"You must be wondering why I stay with her."

"No. I envy her enthusiasm."

"She's the most exciting thing that's ever happened to me." He turned toward her, leaning against the wooden rail. "And crazy as it sounds, the leaving is part of it."

"Of the excitement?"

"Yes." He took a sip from the plastic tumbler. His eyes, she saw, were brown. "I must sound masochistic." He laughed.

"I never thought of leaving as exciting." She leaned on the rail beside him. "Scary, maybe."

"Scary. Exciting." He shrugged.

"Don't you worry that she's gone? For good?"

"I did the first time. Nearly went mad. Didn't know what I had for her, what possible reason she would find to come back."

"And now you do?"

"No." He shook his head. "I have no idea. But she does come back. Reason or no reason."

Half of the sun was still visible, but the docks below were dark. Kate pulled her sweater onto her arms and shook her head. "Running off into Mexico that way: strange country, different language. She's not afraid of much, is she?"

"She doesn't need much, either. It gives her a certain freedom."

"And yet she married you."

He laughed. "Actually, she didn't. We were just playing to the audience." He glanced down at her, eyes crinkling. "Not you. The old ones."

She smiled at his gallantry. She felt quite safe with him.

Most of the other passengers had gone for drinks or to change for dinner, but Kate and Robert stayed at the rail until the last streaks of sun were gone.

"How long since your husband died?" he asked.

"About a year," she said.

He glanced at her. "It must have been terrible for you."

She took a breath. "He had a heart attack, and his car went off the road." She looked up at him. "At first they thought he'd been impaired, or careless." She shook her head. "Not my Will."

"He was young for a heart attack."

She nodded. "Forty three." She sighed and took a sip. "Young. Yes. It seemed that way at the time."

"Kids?"

She shook her head.

She wanted to ask him what it did to the air, the strain between him and Carla before she left him. Whether he could feel it coming, how it made him feel.

"Well, this," he said, waving his hand up at the string of lights and flags that ran from the mast to the deck, "is a sign that you're recovering." He smiled, obviously warmed by the thought.

She shrugged. "It's a sign that his family's recovering. They thought this would be perfect."

"But it isn't."

She looked out in the direction of the land – of Mexico – but it was too dark to see it any more. "Depends on what they had in mind."

He asked her if she wanted to go dancing after dinner.

"I don't think so," she said, surprised.

She thought about the casinos, the lounges, the floor shows and the bars. Thought about her cabin, being alone in it again.

"How about a game of Scrabble?" she said.

"Perfect," he said. "We'll play for drinks."

~

They took the same tender from the ship to the dock in Puerto Vallarta, and they sat together on the bus.

Kate admired stone arches at the waterfront, and Robert was able to add detail to the guide's patter: Carla wasn't the only one who'd been doing research. They were scornful when the bus stopped to show them Elizabeth Taylor's house, but Kate got out and took a picture because she knew Eleanor would enjoy it. Later, when they were given a drink in an outside bar at an expensive new hotel, Kate was stunned by the colours of the bougainvillea that hung from the balconies. Robert made sure she noticed the bar stools, too, pedestals in the water of the pool. Planted on top of them were burned tourists, wearing skimpy bathing suits the colours of Mexico's flowers.

At their shopping stop, she bought a straw hat with a colourful band for Eleanor, and some note paper that said Hecho in Mexico on it for herself. Robert bought a turquoise-and-silver necklace for Carla.

"Same colours as the mirachi band on board," he said, amused, showing it to her. "Carla was quite taken with that band." He seemed so cheerful, unperturbed by her absence.

When they got back to the ship, Kate noticed that her skin was pink. That night, she suggested that they dance.

They wandered under waterfalls at Ixtapa's newest hotel, through the gardens of a half-built city, then sat outside while the others visited the shops. It was the time of the siesta, and not all the stores were open. This angered a few of the passengers, but the tour guide kept smiling. "You shop in Xijuatenejo," he said. "After we get back." His smile looked thin.

Kate thought of the hawkers on the docks at Xijuatenejo, loaded down with hats and dresses and silver-coloured chains. "Lady, you buy! Lady?" She wondered where they put their goods at night. She imagined heaps of silver chains and sombreros and long scarves in the corners of small dark rooms. Rooms protected by concrete walls with glass spikes across the top.

"Something to be said for government intervention," Robert said, looking around him at the resort city the state had created a few miles away from the poorer Xijuatenejo, which was the port and had been the original town.

It was the kind of thing Will might have said. She felt the familiar jolt of anger at being left by him the way she had, an anger that gave her hands nothing to close on but themselves. And then came the familiar guilt.

"I don't feel like I'm even seeing Mexico," she said suddenly. "All we've seen is hotels and shopping centres."

Another tour bus had arrived and the Munroes and the Murrays descended from it together.

"If you wanted to see Mexico, you should have gone to Mexico," Robert told her.

Mr. Munroe noticed Robert and Kate and waved his hand in greeting. This attracted the attention of the others, who also gave little waves. Kate and Robert waved back. The Munroes and Murrays did not approve of them, and their meals had become quite formal.

"This is all of Mexico these people want to see," Robert said.

"And you?"

"It's a holiday. I don't have to make decisions, and I don't have to worry about the food."

She leaned back and closed her eyes. The sun and the drink had made her sleepy.

"Never mind," he said. "You're turning brown. When you get home it will look as though you've been to Mexico, even if you haven't."

~

Kate was up early, dressed and outside as the ship drew into the harbour at Acapulco. Although it was not quite six, the sun was hot on her arms.

The bay was blue and calm, the houses and apartments of the city set into the hills like pale paste jewels. Kate looked across at a huge white cross standing on a hill and knew the tour bus would not go near it. Instead, it would take them down the coast to exclusive hotels where they'd be given drinks, and then it would take them back to a shopping centre where they'd be given more drinks, and time. Tomorrow, Robert and the Murrays and the Munroes would leave the ship, and a whole new set of dinner companions would join Kate for the trip back north.

The night before she'd said, "I wanted to leave my husband. For five years, I'd been this close to it." In the dark she'd held her thumb and forefinger a centimetre apart. "But I never went through with it."

"That makes it worse," he'd said, understanding right away.

"I was afraid to be alone." She laughed, feeling near to tears. "Ironic, isn't it? But I didn't have the nerve that Carla does."

He looked down at her. "Would you have gone back to him?"

"I don't think so."

She felt the ship lunging forward, down the coast of Mexico, moving them quickly through the night.

"It's harder to leave if it's permanent," he said.

She wondered how he knew that.

He'd held her, waiting for her to cry, but she found she didn't need to. She'd told somebody, and that seemed to be enough for now. She pressed her lips against his shoulder and felt glad, for this moment, to be right where she was.

Now she felt him come up behind her and put one hand around her waist. She turned and smiled and he handed her a coffee he'd brought for her. Acapulco was beautiful, she told him. He kissed her on the forehead and wandered off toward the bow.

As they approached the dock, she leaned against the rail and looked down at the water.

"Robert!" she called.

He came and stood beside her.

Far below them, children were swimming out to the ship, very thin, bare-chested boys in shorts. A woman not far away from Robert threw a coin to them, and the boys dove as the coin hit the water. More coins followed, thrown from along the decks, and the boys dove and dove. Kate closed her eyes.

"They swim too close," Robert said. He looked at the woman who'd thrown the coin and said more loudly, "Some of them have been killed."

The woman, angry rather than ashamed, moved away. Kate stepped back so she couldn't see the water.

"Do they do it to get money for themselves? Their families?"

"Who knows? Undoubtedly they're poor."

"So poor they're not afraid to die?"

"I doubt they think about it. Kids figure they're invulnerable. It's us aging comfortable types who interpret things as dramatic." He laughed. "Not that you're aging, of course." He took a sip from his cup. "Or comfortable, after what you've been through."

"I'm comfortable enough for now," she said.

She could see the city better now: a nearly empty park, an avenue filled with early morning traffic, dilapidated panel trucks and buses, and the surprising number of Volkswagen Beetles she'd also noticed in the other cities they'd visited in Mexico.

The dock itself was busy with men who'd come to attend to the ship's arrival, and already the hawkers were beginning to gather beyond the white customs building. She leaned into Robert's shoulder as the city came up to her: its hotels, its beaches, the heat of its sun.

If she lowered her lids a little, Acupulco looked the way it should to a tourist, like treasure spilled onto the hills by Spanish galleons. With her eyes half-closed and leaning back, she could put the boys out of her mind. She could stop thinking about what all of them up here must look like. All of them up here on this huge, glittering, white, cruise, ship. Throwing pennies.

Robert's arm dropped from her. She opened her eyes and turned to see him leaning against the rail, peering toward the end of the dock. She looked down too, and saw Carla striding out from the customs building.

It could be no one else but Carla. She was wearing something peach and flowing, sandals, a wide-brimmed straw hat with a piece of pink chiffon tied around it, its ends hanging down her back. Kate felt her heart lift just before it sank.

Carla moved briskly toward the ship. She had one hand up to hold her hat on, the chiffon lifting from the breeze she made with her fast walk, and she was squinting at the upper decks. Robert raised his hand. She saw him and began to wave, happily, frantically, bouncing on her toes.

He looked at Kate. "You want to come along? We could spend the day together."

She shook her head. He hugged her but she pushed him off, and in a moment he was gone.

As though she had been heavily clad, in bolts of silk and strands of gold perhaps, and then stripped bare, she shivered.

She took a sip of coffee.

The brown-skinned boys had clambered up onto the dock as the ship edged up against it. They ran across its breadth and dove into a water-filled ditch on the other side. Kate could see a skim of oil floating on its surface.

"Lady! Lady!" they called far below at Carla, diving and twisting in the oily water. Carla didn't seem to hear them. She stood waiting, her eyes on the blue bay.

After a long time, almost half an hour, Robert came out from the shadow of the ship. Carla was sitting on a bench. When he reached her, he put down his bags and pulled her to her feet and put his arms around her. She leaned back to look at him, then hugged him back enthusiastically.

Robert looked up and waved at Kate, and she waved back. He said something to Carla and then she, too, looked up and gave a salute to Kate.

The two of them headed for the customs house and a little while later emerged. Out on the street, they put Robert's things into the trunk of a battered blue Volkswagen Beetle.

Kate watched the car make its way up the long avenue, passing in front of a grey and brown stone building that might have been a fort at some point. It seemed no more than a moment before the car, and Carla and Robert, were gone.

Men, Boys, Girls, Women

Anne has driven more than 1,200 kilometres to get to the coast and beyond. She has swerved around sheep which wandered onto the highway near Cranbrook and she's left strips of rubber in Creston, where she narrowly missed a cyclist. Near Trail she hurtled down the side of a mountain in the fog, pursued by a semi-trailer which had lost its brakes. Still, it hasn't occurred to her to worry about the car until this moment.

She is leaning against the trunk of a fir tree on the heights of Bluff Park, watching the Vancouver ferry start into Active Pass and waiting for the bellow of its horn. It has begun to drizzle, and she's moved against the tree for shelter. Although she is dressed for walking, she has not prepared for rain.

She's been thinking how different the ferry looks from above – no more significant than a boat in a bathtub – than it does from a passenger's perspective. Inside that vast, shuddering vessel, she's wandered from the aluminum and glass and arborite of the cafeteria past the souvenir and news stand, through wide-windowed rooms with rows and rows of upholstered seats, past card tables and video games and the snack shop, up to the salt-streaked window at the bow. Then, she has had the sense that it is the landscape that is moving. The ferry is fixed and permanent. The water and the islands are the drifters.

It was like that in the car as they moved toward the coast. The station wagon was a piece of home, their juice cans and empty chip bags strewn across its floor mats, suitcases and shoulder bags where they'd thrown them in the back. They could put their hands on their possessions in an instant, could stop and in a moment change into an entirely different set of clothes as familiar as the ones already on their backs. Surrounded by their books, their magazines, they became settlers of a kind. What of the mountains, the villages and parks? The bridges and railroad tracks, the cliffs and channels? Those were the novelties, gone within the moment. Those things moved past the windows of their little stockpile, reeled themselves out alongside their familiar place.

After twelve years, the blue station wagon is as familiar as a car can get. Every spring and winter and the few times when it's broken down, she's taken it to the service station near where she lived when she was married. The owner there does not embarrass her about her lack of knowledge about cars. He explains carefully what needs to be done and why, and she reads his work orders with attention before she signs them. He is a small soft man of nearly sixty years, no taller than her shoulder, his hair white and his nails ridged with black. She advises him about RRSPs and mutual funds, and they are satisfied with their respective areas of expertise.

For the weekend, she has left the car and the children in Victoria with her mother and her father. She's come over to Galiano for some solitude, after months of work and children, and after the long drive.

She begins the five-kilometre walk back to L'Auberge, the small inn where she is staying. She stops at the bottom of the hill at the edge of the park to watch a water plane land near the ferry dock, and then she starts down the highway. She keeps close to the edge of the pavement for the shelter of the trees. It is raining harder now.

When they arrived from the ferry at her parents' home, her mother gathered all three of them, in the driveway, in a hug. Anne looked over at her father, and found him a little thinner than he used to be, but not much changed from the last time she had seen him. He was walking around her car and examining its rust spots.

Eddie broke from the women and went to stand beside his grandfather. He was now taller than Anne's father, and beginning to fill out. He, too, studied the rust that was eating away the lower body of the station wagon.

"My dad's just got a new Toyota," he said.

"Toyota's a good car," Anne's father replied.

Later that night, when Jess and Eddie were asleep, he came into the kitchen.

"Let me lend you money for a car," he said.

There was a pause while Anne's mother looked at Anne, then at Anne's father, her face expressionless, her breath held, her hand still over Anne's where she'd just been patting it and saying how glad she was that they had come.

The pause was not one in which Anne made up her mind. There was no question of what she'd say. She was remembering that this was the way he did things. She put him back into context in that pause, remembering other things he'd offered in the years since her divorce: a lawn mower, lift-out windows, a gas barbeque, new roofing. And then she shook her head.

She felt her mother's hand squeeze hers.

"Thanks anyway," she said to her father, who'd already shrugged and gone to pour the water for his pills.

"Any time you need it," he said. "It wouldn't put us short."

"I know."

Her mother said, "She'll get a car when she wants to, Neil. Anne is doing fine."

When she gets back to the inn, she changes into dry clothes and goes downstairs for dinner. She is shown to a table for two near the window, and she sits so that her back is to the other tables in the dining room. There was a time when she felt uncomfortable at the way her aloneness called attention to her in dining rooms and restaurants. People avoided looking at her, as though she had a strawberry birth mark on her face or had forgotten to wear a blouse. But she's learning not to worry about what other people think, and tonight she's feeling peaceful after the walk. She's looking forward to bouillabaisse and sole, and to the warmth of wine.

But she finds herself looking through the rain on the window at the cars in the small parking lot. Gleaming from the light at the top of the pole near the inn, they all look new and reliable. As though the confines of the island have compressed them, most of them are small, much smaller than her own old, ship-like, rust-eaten vehicle. Hers, she decides, is the kind of car that stalls for no apparent reason in intersections and on highways. And passersby think, What did she expect?

~

"You had a lot of rain," her mother says when she gets back. "It's too bad." Her mother is pleased with herself for giving Anne a break, and she doesn't want to think that her rest has been spoiled in any way.

"It was fine," Anne assures her. "The weather didn't matter."

Her parents have taken her children everywhere while she's been gone. They've been to Sealand, the wax museum, the Empress Hotel for tea. They have saved the Butchart Gardens for Anne's return and for an improvement in the weather. When it comes, Anne wants to drive them out in her car: it's been sitting by the curb since she arrived and she's been thinking about it almost constantly since Galiano. The more she thinks about it, the less familiar and reliable it seems.

But her parents won't hear of it, so she squeezes into the back seat of the Datsun between her son and daughter, both of them nearly the size of adults, and as they drive the crossroads and byways of Brentwood, she listens to the steady hum of the engine of her father's car.

In the gardens, Eddie and his grandfather are soon far ahead of the women. After a few minutes, Jess runs to catch up with them. Anne's mother takes her time, admiring the flowers and telling Anne their names.

"Jennie Butchart's husband moved her all the way out here from Ontario, did you know? He needed limestone for his cement, and this was the place to get it. But she's the one who built the gardens, not him."

"A hobby. Something to keep her mind off being homesick."

"Oh, no," Anne's mother says. "She made the place hers, didn't she? In spite of him. Renovated the Island to suit her taste. Built the gardens right over his limestone quarries. He was finished with them by then, but still...." She smiles. "He had torn up the ground; she restored it. Made it even more beautiful than it was before."

Anne's mother looks for such subtle acts of independence. Her acceptance of Anne's divorce and her conviction that Anne can make it on her own have numbered among her own small gestures of rebellion.

"If you had been making the decisions," Anne asks her, "would you have moved out here?"

Her mother stops on the path to think about it. "I don't know," she says after a minute. She looks up at Anne with her clear blue eyes. "If I'd been making the decisions, I'd have been a different person, wouldn't I? Not the sort of woman your father would have married, that's for certain." She shrugs. "Or one who'd have married him." She takes a breath and looks away. "We planned all our lives to move out here when he retired. It became inevitable."

They walk along a little farther. The gift shop is ahead. Eddie,

Jess and Anne's father are sitting on a bench, not talking to one another.

Anne's mother suddenly laughs. "Maybe you were just asking if I'm happy here." As though to answer this, she walks ahead and tells Jess and Eddie she'll buy them ice-cream cones.

~

Three days before Anne needs to be back at the office, they catch the ferry to Vancouver. As they are parting, Anne's father says to Eddie, "You're a young man now. You look after them."

Eddie answers, straightening, "Don't worry, sir. I'll make sure we get home safe."

"And so will I," adds Jess, a little miffed.

But they shed maturity and politeness as the ferry leaves the Swartz Bay terminal, pestering Anne for change for snacks and video games and magazines and wanting to know how long the trip will take. They'd rather fly, they tell her, than spend three days in the car.

As the ferry churns its way through the Active Pass Anne, momentarily alone, looks up at the bluffs where she stood in the rain, and thinks about the station wagon on the car deck under them. Given an excuse that her children would buy (a meeting or a death) she would abandon the car in an instant. It no longer feels familiar, or reliable.

But she's been telling them for months that the journey is as important as the destination. It was the lesson she had in mind when she planned this trip, maps and brochures spread out around her after the children were in bed. The trip had expanded with her daring. Not only would she drive to the coast, she would take unusual routes, see places she'd never seen. At Quesnel on the way back, they would make a half-day side trip to see Barkerville, the gold-rush town. She'd create a series of experiences they would not forget, memories they'd share long after they'd moved off into their separate lives.

On the freeways that take them out of Vancouver, she listens to the sounds the car makes, memorizing, monitoring. She should have paid attention before now. In the back seat, Eddie is pestering Jess, and Jess is fighting back. Anne wants to listen to the car, and she threatens to pull to the side of the road if they aren't silent. By the time they reach Hope, the car is a tight container of their irritation.

At a service station, she tells the attendant to check the oil, the brake fluid, the spark plugs, the power-steering fluid, anything he can think of, and then immediately grows irritated with him, too. He's not much older than Eddie. What does he know? He is summer help, young and inexperienced.

"And check the tires," she snaps at him.

He looks up in surprise.

She can take the Coquihalla out of here, cut nearly a day from the drive. She can join the companionship of the cavalcade of vans and motor-homes and cars going through the Rogers Pass to Calgary.

~

Instead, she drives north with her teeth clenched. She doesn't want to stop to let them eat, or run, or go to the bathroom. She is irritated when she needs to stop for gas. She wants to keep on driving, all day, all night, until she gets to Edmonton. She believes that a car, this car, this alien vehicle, is more likely to continue moving once it's started than if she allows it to grow cold. When they stop at dinner time, her jaw and her shoulders ache from the way her teeth have been clamped together.

There's a pool at the motel, and the kids are in it before they've even unpacked the car. Anne looks at the bags in the back of the station wagon, and takes out only the one with the scotch in it. She pours herself a drink and sits in the motel room, the door opened onto the grass, onto the shout and splash of pool.

She will learn more about the landscape they've passed through from Jess's photographs than she will from memory. All day she's kept her eyes on the road, her ears on the engine. She slapped away Jess's hand when she tried to turn on the radio.

Despite her weariness, she cannot sleep. When Jess, in the bed with her, finally grows still and Eddie at last stops tossing, she gets up and pulls her jeans and a sweatshirt on. She slips out of the front door and gets into the car, turns on the ignition and listens to the steady running of the engine. She looks at the mountains in the distance and at the moon rising over them. This town offers their last access to the major highway going east.

So what, she asks herself, if I make it home without a problem? I'm not having a good time. I am doing this to prove I can, and not because I want to.

But still she must press on. After Cache Creek the road is emptier and, aside from the truckers, much of the traffic is local. Tired, today Anne stops at any excuse, closing her eyes as she rests on park benches and the kids run and swing and eat. Stopping is preferable to moving now; towns make her feel secure after the exposure of the highway.

The semis that pass her on the highway are so huge and travel such enormous distances, she thinks. Qualified mechanics must check them all the time. She remembers the semi-trailer near Trail, so close against her car that she could have read the writing on it if she hadn't been so frightened. She'd steered down the twisting roadway, praying for a run-off or the entrance to a park, but for miles and miles there had been nothing but the shoulder, too narrow and gravelled to pull onto, to pull away from the huge beast with its hot breath bearing down behind her.

She begins to wonder whether the driver did that on purpose, to scare her, to amuse himself. She feels violated and vulnerable.

At Quesnel, she goes straight past the turnoff to Barkerville. If Eddie and Jess remember the side trip she had planned, they say nothing. She is losing her nerve and she knows it.

"I wish we hadn't come," Eddie says when she snaps at him again. "This has been the worst holiday of my life."

They are driving up a long hill through Prince George and she is watching signs.

Anne takes a deep breath. "We'll probably never get another chance...."

"Who cares," says Eddie. "Who the fuck cares."

~

When at last they turn onto Highway 16, the road that is also wired down at Jasper and then again in Edmonton, Anne begins to feel a little better. The terrain is bleak and rugged, but the nearly deserted road is wide and smooth, and she rapidly puts miles and miles behind them. The hills are becoming larger, becoming mountains in a grey and distant haze, as the moon climbs up into the dusk. She points out ravens, and a coyote standing in the trees. She begins to whistle. Eddie and Jess are quiet, tired of the car and mistrustful of her sudden cheer.

Then, as they start up a long incline, the engine hesitates.

"Don't say a word," Anne warns.

"We didn't," Jess says.

"I told you to be quiet."

Heart pounding, she's gripped the steering wheel tightly, her back ramrod straight and touching the seat only at the bottom of her spine.

Near the top of the slope, the engine hesitates again, making the whole car shudder. And then again.

That was closer to the second than the first, she thinks. Though her mind seems blank, she realizes she's timing them, like labour pains. She knows about labour pains, knows about mortgages and T-bills, knows about eating alone in restaurants. She knows nothing about cars.

"Something's wrong," Eddie says flatly from the back.

"Clever," Jess says.

Anne tells them to shut up, shut up, shut up so she can listen. In fact, she doesn't want to listen, doesn't want to hear. Doesn't want to be alone out here on the darkening highway with a car that doesn't work. And she is alone, she knows it. She is the one who must make the decisions that will take them out of the bush, away from these mountains, home. Jess's and Eddie's concerns are small, disproportionate to hers and to reality: they suppose she will take care of them.

She starts down the hill, and she can see in the moonlight other hills and others after that. They pass a sign which says "McBride – 80 km." It lists places after, Dunster, Tête Jaune Cache, but nothing before.

The car hesitates again. The only way to keep her hands from shaking is to keep them on the wheel.

For long minutes, the car continues to run, hesitating on a basis too irregular for her to interpret it. Just when she thinks the problem's gone, it comes again. A pickup truck goes by the other way. She wishes there were a way to flag a driver down, but she doesn't want to stop. Her car has shown itself at last, turned against her, trapping her inside it.

But that is stupid, she tells herself. It is just a car. Things fit into other things and make it run. She cards her memory for other times when it has behaved like this, to put a diagnosis on these symptoms, but can remember none. It runs strongly between its hesitations. The gas gauge is at the half-way mark.

"I have to pee," Jess says.

They have been keeping low, more wary of her tension than the problems of the car: neither has said a word in several minutes. Grateful, Anne takes a breath.

"You'll have to wait," she says.

"How long?"

"Until we stop," she says. She does not say 'McBride'.

The next hesitation is more than that. Anne pumps the gas but it does no good. The car is slowing. She pulls onto the shoulder of the deserted highway, ready to pull out again if the engine catches, steadies. It doesn't.

Losing power, the car slows on the shoulder. The engine dies. They roll to a stop, Anne still pumping the gas pedal, getting no response. When the car has come to a stop she turns the key. The engine makes a ripping, grinding sound. She turns the car off, and the lights, and puts on the four-way flashers.

"I need to pee," Jess says again.

Anne wants to cry. Instead she says, "Get out and do it, then."

"It's dark. There are bears out there."

"And wolves," Eddie says.

Anne is certain they are right.

"You go with her," Anne says to Eddie.

"I don't want him to come with me. I want you to come with me." Jess is petulant, using a baby voice. You are my mother, that voice says. Protect me. Save me and look after me.

They go together, Eddie wandering a little distance off and turning his back to them. Jess goes to the bottom of the ditch and squats. Anne stands beside her, a box of Kleenex in her hand. It is hard to be a female in the bush. Anne realizes she needs to go, too, then pushes away the thought. She's in charge. She cannot crouch. She looks up at the car while she waits for her children. She cannot crouch, or cry, or appear to sweat.

This is such a silent, empty place. A dark and empty place. A cloud has covered the moon and the highway is edged with dark stains of trees and she can see shapes of mountains in the distance. Nothing moves. Aside from the flashers on her car, which mock her with their illusion of safe passage, there is no light.

Now lights appear on the horizon, high up: a truck. Anne runs stumbling up the slope and stands in front of her car, lit by the flashers, waving. The semi-trailer whizzes past, not slowing. In a minute, it's disappeared. Another zooms past in the opposite direction.

"I hate truckers," Anne says as they get back in the car.

"We going to sit here all night?" Eddie asks from the back seat.

"We may." She is reduced to that, to sitting. Powerless.

Jess and Eddie begin to argue over who ate the last of the crackers. Anne wants to hit them, wants to be a kid and hit them both and let someone bigger, older, save them all.

If she'd told her mother about the trucker who'd amused himself by riding down the mountain on her tail, her mother would have offered the incident shape and meaning and made it into story. Her mother would have said that Anne had brought them safely down, despite the threat, that her capable driving and her calm had brought them through it.

Anne had hurtled down that mountain, mindless with fear, and only luck had kept them alive. If the car had hesitated there, it would have been the end. But her mother would have seen what was nothing more than instinct as an act of courage and independence.

If her mother were here right now, Anne would tell her that Jenny Butchart's gardens were not a political statement. She would tell her that her stories were illusions made of nothing more than smoke, blown away in an instant.

Now in her rearview mirror she sees headlights, approaching more slowly, much more slowly than the last ones. A truck pulls off the highway, a huge Mack cab which draws a trailer after it, its headlights beaming hard into their car. It stops, with a sigh of brakes, so close behind them Anne can see the insects smashed against its grill. Her heart begins to pound.

Leaving his lights on, the engine running, a man in blue jeans and a camouflage vest jumps down from the cab.

"Lock your doors," Anne says, hearing her voice sound thin.

"Why?" says Jess, surprised.

"Just do it."

The man comes to her window and she rolls it down an inch.

"Problem?" he asks. He is heavily built, muscular, tall and blond. Mid to late twenties. Women, she thinks, are notches on his belt.

"The car," she says. "Won't go." She gropes for words that will make her sound less helpless. Finds none. "It isn't out of gas."

"You want to try it?"

"We'll be all right," she says.

But she does try it, she has no choice, and the car starts immediately and runs steadily for a moment before it falters. Stalls.

He asks her to try again. This time it won't turn over. He tells her to pop the hood, his voice commanding, taking charge. She does. He walks around to the front. He raises the hood. Through the space between the hood and the car, she can see him lifting caps from wells. She hates him. She hates sitting here.

Before she realizes what he's doing, Eddie is out of the car and around the front, standing beside the truck driver. She calls to him to come back, but he ignores her.

The man goes back to the truck and returns with a plastic jug. He pours its contents into one of the wells in the engine. He talks to Eddie and Eddie talks back to him. Anne cannot hear their words. She hates sitting while they stand.

After a few minutes, he calls her to try the car again. She does.

It hesitates, then starts. It keeps running, steadily. The man throws the plastic jug into the ditch, slams down the hood and comes back to her window. Eddie comes with him.

"What did you do?" she asks.

He shrugs. "Windshield fluid. Noticed you were low."

"That doesn't affect the engine."

"No," he says. "Kills time."

Eddie says, "He thinks it was dirt in the gas line."

The man nods. "Can't trust the gas, some of these places. I'll follow you to town."

"Can I ride with him?" Eddie asks.

"No," Anne says sharply. "You get in."

The trucker chucks Eddie on the shoulder and starts away.

He does follow her into McBride, his lights too close behind her. Anne is tense until they reach the edge of town. As she pulls into a service station, the trucker flashes his lights and zooms past, down the highway toward Edmonton.

She stops the car at the doors to the service bay and puts her hands up to her face.

Eddie gets out and talks to the attendant. The two stand looking at the car, deep in conversation. Anne thinks that it is magic that Eddie is learning tonight, the incantations that make cars go. She will never know them.

~

When the bags and suitcases are in the motel room and Eddie and Jess have disappeared to find the pool, Anne phones Victoria.

Her father is surprised to hear her voice. "Everything all right?" he asks.

"Sure. We're in McBride."

"How is the motel?"

"It's fine."

"We've stayed there. Not fancy, but it's clean. And safe." He clears his throat. "Trip going okay?"

"Of course."

She can't tell her father what has happened. He'll want to buy her a new car. He'll want to speak to Eddie. Later, he'll tell her mother that if Anne were married, these things wouldn't happen.

It's her mother she wants to talk to. But secure in the knowledge that Anne is at the wheel and getting them all safely home, her mother has gone out to a neighbour's to play bridge.

Annie lies down on one of the beds after she's hung up the phone, and closes her eyes. After a while, she is able to imagine her car back on the highway, its engine dead, in the middle of the dark, in the middle of the bush. She sees it as if she were on a cliff above it. She can see the highway for miles in each direction and this car, this blue station wagon, is the only vehicle on it. Its yellow flashers blink and blink.

Three people are inside the car, a woman and two children. The engine of the car is dead, and the woman must find a way to get the children home.

Slowly now, and very carefully, Anne begins to build this story on her own.

Show Jumping

June knew that her husband was falling in love with Krista before he did. At first, it was not anything specific about the way he acted or anything he said, but rather an unusual buoyancy in him that was practically contagious.

Krista was Gregory's research assistant. She was both intelligent and young. She'd gone into her master's program directly following a B.Sc., which led June to conclude that she was likely inexperienced in the ways of the world. Sort of like Gregory, when she thought of it. June was not, herself, so innocent.

He called about noon one warm Sunday late in May to ask what June thought of going to the equine centre.

"Just for an hour or so," he said. "They've got a show down there – mostly kids apparently. Nothing professional. I thought it might be fun to have a look."

He'd gone over to the university at nine, saying he didn't think he'd be home until dinnertime. It was so unlike him to propose an outing, especially when it would interrupt his work, that June found the phone call disturbing. She almost said, "No," just to keep him at the university where he belonged.

But when he'd called, she'd been sitting at the coffee table in the kitchen, staring out the window into the garden, a stack of unread manuscripts at her elbow. The day was clear and hot, and she'd been wishing she were at the lake house instead of in the city.

"Good, then," Gregory said. "We'll pick you up in half an hour."

"We?"

"Krista," Gregory said, as though surprised he hadn't mentioned her. "Her sister's jumping in the show."

With uncharacteristic punctuality, Gregory pulled up the driveway exactly thirty minutes later. Krista smiled a greeting at June as she gave up her seat in the front and moved into the back.

Gregory glanced at June as he backed out of the driveway. "Did I tell you Krista's sister's in the show?"

"You did." June turned a little, doing up her seat belt. "Do you ride as well?"

"Yes," Krista said, shifting across the back seat, perhaps so June could see her better. "I don't compete any more, but I do still ride when I can find the time."

~

June had never been to the equine centre. She'd admired it often on her way to work, a pleasant stretch of green in the middle of the city. The stables were visible from Park Drive, but the competition area was concealed from the freeway by a number of grassy knolls. It would be nice to have a closer look.

It was as they were walking from the parking lot that June first became aware that she felt like the odd one out. Without meaning to, she didn't think, Krista and Gregory had fallen into step with one another and were walking up the hill ahead of her.

She watched the two of them, Gregory's head inclined a little toward Krista's. In the car, they'd been talking about some pellets they'd been analyzing. Gregory's current research concerned the eating patterns of the Northern Saw-Whet Owl.

June had met Krista before, but she'd never really looked at her.

Now that she did, she found her rather oddly proportioned. Her legs were quite long in comparison with her torso, and this made her look taller than she was – which was almost the same height as Gregory. She was slender, with dark curly hair, and she wore glasses. There was something attractive about her look – neat, compact, and slightly scholarly, even in the walking shorts and T-shirt she was wearing that afternoon.

She walked up the hill briskly, and Gregory strode along beside her. He was overdressed in his long-sleeved white shirt, his grey trousers, his grey socks. Sandals were the only concession he'd made to the approach of summer.

Gregory was June's second husband. She'd been married to him five years now, and in that time his dark brown hair and beard, still thick and full, had greyed considerably, and the lines on his face had deepened. In certain men, the passage of time seemed of itself to produce an appearance of substance and validity, and Gregory was one of those.

His expression was often one of intense curiosity, as though the answer to a question he'd been mulling over all his life was now within his grasp – would be provided, in fact, by the very person with whom he was now speaking. Knowing, as June did, that he was often not even listening to the other person made this expression somewhat less appealing, but there was no doubt at the moment that he was listening to Krista.

June reached the top of the hill. Below her, there were two large rings surrounded by white railings. In one, a rider was jumping her horse over low green fences. At a distance, between where June stood and the stables, was a high structure where the announcers and the judges sat. Beyond them, a row of white flags waved in the warm breeze.

By the time June reached Gregory and Krista, they were settled near the area where riders and horses awaited their turns on the course. Gregory had pulled out his pipe and was filling it as June sat down beside Krista.

"Krista started to ride when she was five," he said, tamping the tobacco. "Her sister was even younger."

"Remarkable," June said. She nodded at the course. "How old are these riders?"

"Fourteen, fifteen or so," Krista said. "Deirdre's seventeen. She's on a little later."

"Deirdre is Krista's sister," Gregory said.

June watched one rider after another essay the course, some more successfully than others. Gregory asked a question now and then about the competition, but most of the time he and Krista talked about undigested fur and insect exoskeletons. Gregory grew enthusiastic as they talked, and Krista seemed as interested as he was.

June was surprised at his energy in the heat until she recognized the symptoms. It was like she wasn't there. A woman nearby looked over at Krista and Gregory, curious at their conversation, and then looked at June beside them.

June, who'd been thinking about Alan and the others, smiled at her – then nodded. She wasn't sure why she'd nodded, but it seemed to confuse the woman, and she looked away.

~

Gregory had gone to find them something cold to drink but he had been held up, and he started back around the course just as Deirdre was announced to start her ride. He turned to watch, three plastic cups gathered in his hands.

June felt Krista tense as Deirdre started out, pull back as she approached each fence, and then relax as the horse and rider cleared it. Deirdre had been over earlier to talk to them, and June had noticed that she was built like Krista – short torso, relatively long legs – although they didn't otherwise look much alike. Because of her build, Deirdre looked younger in the saddle than she did up close.

She completed four jumps smoothly, and seemed to be riding faster than the others in her class. But at the fifth jump her horse balked, and before June even realized what was happening, Deirdre was thrown forward over the fence to the ground, the horse was heading back toward the starting gate, and Krista was on her feet and running down the hill.

At the railing, Krista stopped. The trainer was out already, running toward Deirdre. She'd grabbed the reins of the horse on her way by and the beast trotted along behind her, docile. Deirdre stirred slowly and sat up, keeping her head down. At the trainer's insistence, she finally stood and took the reins, holding one elbow with her hand. To warm applause, she walked her horse back toward the starting gate.

June was watching Gregory. Drinks clutched in his hands, his eyes, bemused and distant, were on Krista as she moved up the hill toward June. He seemed unaware of Deirdre's accident. In his head, June thought, he and Krista were somewhere miles away.

~

June saw that Krista was falling in love with Gregory at a reception for a colleague of Gregory's who was leaving for a year of research in Australia. The gathering was ostensibly to wish the colleague well – which no one, in fact, did.

June was there in her capacity as director of the university press. The Australia-bound professor, a parasitologist, had a contract with them to do a book. Gregory was there as a senior member of his department. It was at a similar gathering that June and Gregory had met.

June was a little surprised when Krista appeared. Master's students didn't normally attend these kinds of things. Gregory, who was standing beside June, lost in thought, didn't seem to notice her arrival.

A few minutes later, Krista arrived at June's side, holding a glass of wine. She was wearing a dark red dress, quite short but smart and obviously expensive.

"You wear clothes like that, and you'll have no future in academics," June said.

Krista looked down at her dress, then up at June, concerned.

June smiled. "It was meant to be a compliment. 'Stodgy' is the look we strive for here."

Krista relaxed and smiled. She glanced at Gregory, her expression open, soft. His look was guarded, but there was no missing the attraction.

"How's your sister?" June asked.

Krista paused as though mulling over the question. Then she said, "Bruised elbow. Nothing serious."

"I'm glad to hear it. Dangerous activity, jumping."

Krista nodded solemnly. "They're trying to make protective equipment mandatory. Helmets, anyway. But riders would rather be fashionable than safe."

Gregory had come to life. "They had the same problem with cyclists once," he said, "and now just look at them. I'm sure it will be the same for horseback riders." He paused and, with a smile at Krista, added, "A helmet wouldn't have helped your sister much."

It wasn't the kind of thing that Gregory would normally have said. People didn't spend enough time studying their own behaviour, June decided. They should. They never knew when they'd need to imitate it.

She, single in those days and feeling mighty in her singleness, had been as concerned as Alan – more, it sometimes seemed – that they not get caught, that neither of them by glance or gesture compromise themselves or one another. She didn't want his marriage to disintegrate. She didn't want any part in causing something like that to happen, and she didn't want to deal with the fall-out if it did. The affair had lasted nearly a year, and they had continued to work together when it was over. As far as she knew, no one in the office had suspected. As far as she knew, he was still married to the woman they had betrayed.

At the time she hadn't thought much about Alan's wife. She had met her only once, and Alan never talked about her. Since the Sunday at the equine centre, she'd been thinking about her a lot.

"People should be allowed to decide for themselves," she said. "Hockey, horseback riding, cycling. If they want to smash their brains to bits, it should be up to them."

Krista looked away. Gregory nodded, then glanced uncomfortably at Krista.

June said to Krista, "I gather you managed to avoid getting injured? When you were competing?"

Gregory looked down at Krista's leg just an instant before she held out her left foot. She said, "I broke my ankle once. That's when I quit." She smiled and raised her eyes to June's. "I'm afraid I lost my courage."

June looked from Krista to Gregory.

"Surely not all of it," she said.

~

June said in the car on the way home, "I didn't expect Krista to be there."

Gregory shrugged. "She's been working pretty hard. I thought she might enjoy it."

"Why should she? No one else did."

He smiled, not looking at her. "There isn't much going on this time of year. I wanted her to meet a few people in the department."

June was feeling steely. Wine did that to her, gave her an exoskeleton of her own, but there was more to it than that. The way she was able to see through them, Krista and Gregory, made her feel scornful and superior.

As they passed the equine centre she said, mainly to see how he'd respond, "Maybe we should invite her to the lake."

"To the lake."

"For dinner." She looked over at him. "With her boyfriend, if she has one."

His brow had furrowed. "Why would we do that?"

"She's a nice young woman. I quite like her." She looked down at her hands. "Why not?"

Gregory said, "I don't think she has a boyfriend."

"Oh," June said, "she must. An attractive young woman like that? Maybe she just hasn't told you."

"I don't think she does," he said quite seriously.

"Well, then. We could invite the kids." Meaning his, and hers. "They're about the same age she is."

"Oh, no," he said. "I don't think so. They're not at all interested in my work." He shifted in his seat. "The Dicksons might be better."

The wine was wearing off, and June was beginning to have misgivings. She'd been certain he'd refuse, but instead he was warming to the idea. He said as he turned into their driveway, "I suppose I could show her where the owls roost."

~

June could not stop thinking about those other wives: Alan's had not been the only one. Now that she was becoming one of them, she thought about them all the time.

She had not considered herself a threat to them. She didn't want their husbands, nor did the husbands want to leave their wives. She'd thought of the affairs as good things, small avalanches of intensity and passion in busy, routine lives. Finished in their time – and with no hard feelings afterward on either side. She had always been careful, fastidiously circumspect. She'd believed they'd left no victims.

But perhaps they had. It had never occurred to her that the wives of these men might have known what was going on from the way their husbands had changed. That no matter what she said or didn't say, what she did or didn't do, these women would find out.

How could they not have known? she wondered now. Decent men, their husbands, men like Gregory. They didn't do that kind of thing. And what had the women said, when they recognized what was happening? How had they behaved? In what domestic dramas had she, unknown to her, been given a starring role?

She glanced over at Gregory. They were on their way to the lake, and the trunk of the car was filled with groceries, beer and wine. There would be eight for dinner. The Halburns were coming, and the Dicksons. Jed Dickson's mother, who was staying at the lake, would make the number even. Krista, it turned out, did not have a boyfriend.

June was driving, Gregory reading *Equinox* in the passenger seat, one knee against the door. He was wearing lake clothes – navy shorts, a grey T-shirt – and the light on the dark hairs above his knee, the shape of the knee itself, made her want to weep.

"Do you think there's something missing from our marriage?" she asked him, keeping her voice steady.

He put his finger on the word he'd last read and looked over at her. "Missing? How?"

"A spark or something. I don't know."

"A spark or something," he repeated. He was still looking at her, genuinely puzzled from the sound of it. She'd noticed that he was getting better at dissembling.

"I don't know," she said.

"Is everything all right?"

"Of course. I was just thinking."

Their relationship had been remarkable in her life because of its lack of turmoil. They had met and courted and finally married on such a low key that it had all seemed as natural as going to sleep. It had been almost too peaceful, she'd sometimes thought. It had been dull and unimaginative. It had occasionally been boring.

Other men, including her first husband, had aroused more passion in her, had been able to take away her appetite, and make her temper ragged. But those more emotional relationships had never been coloured by the kind of despair and fear that marbled her feelings now. It did not seem to June that she had ever really been in love before.

As they pulled through the trees beside the lake Gregory stirred himself, yawned and said, "We should get someone out to look at the roof."

He is planning for the future, June thought, and felt her spirits rise.

He's acting like he's planning for the future, she thought, and felt them sink again.

She looked over at him and remembered that she knew him. He's thinking about the roof, she thought. That's all that he is doing.

He was looking at her evenly. Her throat had tightened and she took a breath to loosen it before she said, "That's a good idea."

~

Krista called at 5:30. She had managed to get lost.

June heard the tenor of Gregory's voice change when he realized who it was. He became bright and attentive, cheerful, as he gave her the directions.

June wondered how she'd make it through dinner when even the sight of the mushrooms she was slicing made her nauseous.

The guests, however, were animated, the evening warm with few mosquitoes. They had their drinks out on the deck, high above the lake, and it was clear from the start it would be a successful party.

Krista looked beautiful. She wore an ivory suit of a loosely woven linen, and she had divested herself of the glasses. She seemed to have acquired an even tan in the weeks since June had seen her last. She was charming and witty, bringing out the best in the other guests – especially the men.

It turned out she was a little older and more experienced than June had thought. She'd travelled for two years following the third year of her baccalaureate program, working on a farm in New Zealand and at a restaurant in Greece. Her travelling companion had stayed behind in England when she'd decided to come home.

"We had nothing in common, really," she said lightly. "He was older than I was. Ready to settle down."

June was doing her best not to drink too much, in order to remember how she normally behaved. She passed out small plates of shrimp and raw vegetables, grateful for the domestic industry that she could carry out by rote.

Just as June was about to ask them to come in for dinner, Krista asked directions to the bathroom. Gregory said he wanted to get Jed an article he'd been reading, and he'd show her where it was. The two of them went into the house.

After several minutes, June went back into the kitchen. She checked through the window that the other guests were occupied, then picked up two clean wineglasses and moved into the doorway to the hall. There she stood still, and listened.

"It's a beautiful place," Krista said, quietly but distinctly.

"I'll show you the boat house after dinner," Gregory said. "There's a family of loons down there."

"That would be wonderful," Krista said in the same measured tone. It was a tone that June knew well, one that said everything but gave nothing away. At least that's what she'd thought at one time.

There was a silence before the bathroom door clicked closed.

June put the glasses on the table in the dining room, then went back to the kitchen and turned on the tap.

Gregory came in and put one hand around her waist. "Great party," he said. "Thanks." He was holding the magazine he wanted to give to Jed, totally unconcerned.

"I shouldn't have invited her," she said suddenly.

"Who?"

"Krista."

"Oh, I think she'd having a good time," he said. "She seems to be fitting in quite well."

Smooth, she thought. You're getting very good at this.

"She has a crush on you," she said softly, and felt him flinch.

She turned, but he'd pulled himself together. "Don't be silly," he said. "A girl her age?"

He gave her a brief hug and went outside.

~

During dinner, Krista and Gregory avoided eye contact. As she put down plates and cleared them, June considered the life that she and Gregory had created with one another, this lake house, these good friends, and wondered how he could risk throwing it away.

But later, in the darkness of the kitchen, she thought that maybe he wasn't risking anything at all – no more than Alan and the others had risked their lives to be with her.

An image of Alan's wife rose up before her, a woman so petite that June had been able to dismiss her from her thoughts for many years.

Maybe it was only the way you saw it – whose eyes you saw it through. Maybe it was up to her this time.

When she came back to the dining room, Jed's mother asked her how she'd made the pie crust, startling her back into the here and now. There was nothing she could do at the moment anyway, except to carry on. She smiled at Jed's mother, and said she'd used a packaged mix.

~

Later, Gregory would take Krista down to the boat house, and he would show her where the loons were, and the tree where an owl liked to roost. At some point June would go outside and stand on the deck in the darkness for a moment, and she would imagine them together – concealed by trees below her, their words muffled, silenced, by moving leaves and the lap of water. By the time they came back up, she would be inside again, occupied with conversation, pouring coffee, clearing away the dishes.

In the same way, she would wait for Gregory – for as long as she needed to, saying nothing before or after.

She would not be alone. She felt them gathering behind her – Alan's wife, and the others. Malevolent? Perhaps. Vindicated, certainly. Still, she found a peculiar and unexpected strength in knowing they were there.

Relatives and Friends

1.

Even inside the airport you can tell it's warmer here than it is back East, the air spring-spongy, fragrant. Sarah sees me first – as quick of eye and wit as I was at her age. She gets it through Uncle Geoff. Not necessarily from Geoff himself, but from our side of the family. Geoff sees me too and now Alicia Mae is turning, slowly, puzzled – having, it appears, expected me to arrive from some other direction. "Where?" "Where?" I can almost hear her saying in her little-girl voice before she catches sight of me on the escalator.

"Em!" Sarah calls, "Em!" – waving across the crowds, and my happiness to see her and the sight of her happiness to see me spread across my face into a smile. She's wearing dark grey tailored trousers, a white blouse and a dust-blue cardigan, and her long pale-brown hair is drawn smoothly back into a pony tail. She's fifteen now, and I am amazed that she still lets herself be dressed this way: that there is still no evidence of her tongue's having been pierced or of tattoo artists having had their way across her wrists.

My heart feels as though it is literally going out to her as I put my arms around her. She holds the hug longer than I expect her to – her hair smells clean and sweet. And then Alicia Mae and I touch lips to cheeks and cheeks to lips: so cool, the two of us – aunt and niece, but not relatives, as neither of us lets the other one forget.

Uncle Geoff runs a hand through his thick grey hair, standing a little distance off and watching us as though he is embarrassed. I noticed this same awkwardness in Toronto three weeks ago, when he came there for a meeting. It was the first sign anything was wrong and now, for the first time in my life, he doesn't greet me with a hug. I feel its absence against my chest and along the insides of my arms, but I let him be.

"Well," I say. "Here we are."

"You're looking very well," says Alicia Mae, her eyes on the hem of my skirt. It isn't hard to imagine what she really thinks about the way I look, so vastly different from what she puts together for herself to admire in the mirror every day. She hasn't changed a single aspect of her appearance since I first met her nearly thirty years ago: she wears a peculiar style that was out of date even back then, when everyone else her age was wearing beads and jeans and fringed vests and tie-dyed bands around their heads, and there she was in these full-skirted chiffon dresses that came just below her knees, high-heeled white sandals, stockings, and her hair pulled back in a chignon.

"So do you," I say.

Today it's a pale blue dress with small white dots, belted at the waist – she's kept her figure, I will give her that – and she's perched a small white hat on her head in honour of the season. She would not stand out in a *Father Knows Best* rerun.

"How was your flight?" she asks me.

"Very smooth. I had a good view of the mountains."

"I'm glad to hear it," she says. "Some people have bad luck up there. With clouds."

"Luggage, Em?" asks Uncle Geoff.

"Just one bag."

"I'll get it," Sarah says, heading off toward the carousel. She knows my luggage, has perched on the edge of the bed in their guest room often enough watching me unpack or pack, asking me about everything I take out or put in.

"You wouldn't need much for a weekend," says Alicia Mae.

"Not much," I say agreeably, "if you knew what to expect in the way of weather."

Alicia Mae sighs and turns to look toward the carousel. "It's a long way to come for a weekend."

"She's got a meeting," Geoff says as though he's speaking to a willfully stupid child. "This is a big country, Alicia. People travel long ways to meetings."

I clear my throat, uncomfortable at his tone, although I must admit to some satisfaction at it, too. She begs to be spoken to that way, and I always feel like doing it myself.

"Nevertheless," she says, looking down at her hands, which are holding her white handbag by the clasp, then looking up and away at nothing.

The effect of her wearing the same type of thing year after year is that it allows you to gauge with ease how much she's aged: it's as though her clothing style is the control group. And she has aged: the lines near her eyes grow deeper every year, and now time is also drawing its fine harrows down the skin above her upper lip. She's not that much older than I am – ten years, that is all. The difference used to seem much greater.

I notice Sarah over by the revolving carousel, gesticulating furiously at my bag and, stepping away from Alicia Mae, I call, "Yes, yes! That's the one!"

She pulls it off the carousel, then hefts it off the floor and onto a luggage cart her father is simultaneously shoving under it.

"Looks heavy," says Alicia Mae behind me.

"Um hmm."

"When's the meeting?"

"Tomorrow afternoon," I say. "At two."

The butterflies lift in my stomach like a disturbance of pigeons on a bridge.

"An unusual time for a meeting," she says.

"An unusual time," I agree.

2.

Cousin Em is telling Dad, and this I can hardly believe – this is going to make him freak completely – that she wants to rent a car. Right now.

"It came to me as the plane was descending through this lovely long wisp of cloud," she says, "how much easier it would be for everyone involved."

She makes it sound as though the idea of renting a car was revealed to her by God or something, but I doubt that even God – which I do not personally believe in – could help her at this point. She didn't hear the two of them last night – my dad with his face about the same colour it is now demanding for my mom to tell him how come if she was coming out here he had to take the whole goddamned afternoon off work and drive all the way back into North Vancouver to get her and then come way out here. Why couldn't she just pick Em up herself? With me, is what he meant. And my mom explaining in this tight little voice that Emmaline is not *her* relative, and if it wasn't for him coming out here to pick her up – with me, she meant: I'd been planning to take a bus from school and meet him at his office – she wouldn't be coming to the airport today at all. As it was, she said, we would do it as a family.

I was scared that something awful might start happening then and there, but my dad just went and slammed himself into his den.

"Now, don't be a silly-billy, Em," Mom says to Cousin Em. "You don't need to rent a car."

Silly billy. Jeez. That's one of those expressions that my father *detests*, which you can see my mom remembering as the words come out of her mouth, looking over at him as she remembers. Sure enough, Dad's face is going redder and again my fear comes up. He wouldn't do it here. Not at the airport. Not in front of Em.

"Dad..." I say, just to remind him where we are.

Em looks at me, then him, then says, "I'm really sorry, Uncle Geoff. I should have thought of it earlier, before you drove all the way out here. But trust me. It'll just be so much easier for everyone if I can get around the city by myself."

"We have two cars," Mom says, her voice wobbling. "*Two* cars, Geoff."

"I insist," Em says, firmly and calmly. "I'm not sure when I'll want to go out, or when I'll be coming back. I'd prefer the freedom not to impose on either of you. It *is* a kind of freedom not to impose. You know that, Geoff. You're a great non-imposer yourself."

I like the way she talks, the way it feels like she's pulling you ahead to catch her meaning, and it's working with him: she's making progress. She looks totally awesome, of course, as usual, which helps.

I'm wishing I hadn't told Heather to come over right away when we get home. I wouldn't mind having Em all to myself for a few hours. Except that Heather just has to see this outfit, which I personally would die for. It's a little black suit with gold buttons, including a row of them down the left side of the skirt, and the skirt is almost as short as the navy plaid one I keep at Heather's place. She's got dark stockings on, which kind of pulls the whole look together – she has great legs – and black suede ankle-high boots that have little gold buttons up them, too. But the best part is that her hair is black this time, as black as midnight, almost purple, like Japanese or Chinese hair, and as silky smooth, and cut as blunt, and she's wearing this funky little black felt tam pulled down over it, lower over her left eye than her right. Amazing.

"What do you want to rent?" my dad says finally.

"Something sexy," Em says, winking at me. "Black."

"I'm not going anywhere this weekend," my mother says. She is walking a little behind us, and when I look back at her, her eyes move from Em's boots to my eyes. I turn back, taking an extra step to catch up to Em.

"I got groceries this morning," she says behind us. "Em can have my car."

Dad says to Mom, "She needs some flexibility, Alicia Mae." Then he says to Em in this light and flirting voice that doesn't sound like him at all and makes me feel gross all over, "You can have sexy-*looking*, but you don't need to go all the way to sexy."

It sounds like he's going to pay for it. Must sound that way to my mom as well – I can feel angry little wires coming out of her without even turning around.

"Can I ride with you?" I ask.

"Of course," Em says, cupping me around the head and pulling me toward her with a smile. She turns to my mom and says, "If that's all right with you."

3.

Far off in the distance I can see the afternoon sun on the city and beyond that the mountains, low, pink, snow-covered. It's been clear the whole way here, all two thousand miles – as clear as I've ever seen it – and then as we start out into the slow wide turn over the Pacific that will bring us back to Vancouver International, there's this one long collie-tail of a cloud – just one – and we come down into it with a bump or two – me with my forehead pressed against the window looking down through a thin white gauze at freighters, yachts and sailboats, at cars and trucks moving like tiny motorized toys along painted-cardboard roads.

It would be nice to have a car here, to be able to skip out at the last minute if I wanted to and drive up to Whistler or out to Harrison Lake instead. Or alternatively – if I'm so inclined – to linger at The Fisherman over a second glass of wine, not feeling I need to cut short a sentence or a glance because I have to get Geoff's car back. Or worse yet, Alicia Mae's.

I need the freedom to get away if I want to. If I need to. Just in case.

The freedom to get away from my family, which is being kind enough to put me up.

Otherwise, I wouldn't be here.

The ocean in the distance is a shining sheet and so clear below us that I can see the continent drop away beneath its surface. Aesthetically speaking, Vancouver's one of the two best cities in the country to start a romance in. Or restart one. If one is so inclined.

"Please ensure that your seat backs and table trays are in the upright position...."

I hope that Uncle Geoff has come out to meet me by himself. It's conceivable, in the middle of Friday afternoon, that he might have come alone. I need to talk to him, to get my bearings before I see Alicia Mae or Sarah. The way he talked last time, I was sure he'd be gone by now.

I'm relieved he isn't gone – where would I stay? – but I'm not surprised he's going. Alicia Mae may have kept her looks, and she can be charming when she wants to, but she is also whiney, helpless, and boring. She talks in this lisping little voice when she wants to get her way, and she's never earned a penny in her life, and she uses silly old-fashioned expressions like "namby pamby" that most of the population's never even heard of any more.

It was as clear that Uncle Geoff was seeing someone when I saw him in Toronto as if he'd had her on his arm. He'd got himself into better trim than he'd been in years – even had a little tan and something in his hair to shine the grey up. He looked vibrant, younger. I guess love can get the hormones going even when you're half way through your sixties. I could feel the difference when he greeted me, in the way it disrupted the usual ease between us, as though he hadn't realized before that night that I was actually a woman.

He told me about her during our second carafe of wine – seemed eager to tell me, proud. She's a corporate lawyer, has done legal work for his company. She's thirty-six – nine years younger than I am! – and divorced. He said he was planning to tell Alicia Mae as soon as he got back. It would be hard for her, but it had to be done and he would pay, "through the nose if necessary." The boys would be fine, he said. Sarah was almost an adult, sensible. He was sure she'd understand.

"Madame? Your table tray."

I hand over my empty coffee cup, push up the tray, lock it into the back of the seat ahead of me. "Thank you."

God knows what a car will cost. I've only got about five hundred left on my VISA card: that's likely to be gone by Sunday no matter what. Couple of sales in the works: if they come through I'll be okay. The nude on the stairs is likely to sell as well – I'll hate to part with it – and the new one, the nude on the chair, if I ever finish it. I've almost got his shoulder the way I want it. Might be done by now, if I hadn't come out here.

I have worried about Sarah in all of this, in spite of what he said. It will be good to see her, to reassure myself that she's all right. At one point, I considered having her east for Easter – east for Easter – but it's so hard to schedule things right now. After all these years, I am finally so close. I have to keep on working.

"Mesdames et messieurs: S'il vous plaît, restez assis jusqu'à ce que l'avion s'arrête au terminal."

There's nothing worse than having someone around that you're obligated to entertain when a creative streak comes on, and there's no knowing when it will happen. I need to be able to work all night or from four to noon or from eight to six these days. I can't afford to block it. I have to be there, ready, when it happens.

I should be there, not here.

I pull my carry-on case out of the overhead bin above my head.

I need my independence. I have to have a car.

4.

"What kind of meeting is it?" I ask her, looking out the window, feeling shy.

"Business," she says lightly, changing lanes. "You know."

"About a sale?" I hope it's about a sale. If it is, it would need to be a big one for her to have flown this far. Maybe it's the break she's been waiting for so long. But she doesn't have any paintings with her. Just a bag. One bag.

Pulling up for a red light, she glances over at me with this kind of sly look in her eyes, then shrugs and looks away. She doesn't want to talk about it, so maybe I've hit it on the head. I'll ask her again later. I'll get it out of her.

I love the way her hair moves when she turns her head.

"Look," she says, her eyes now on the rearview mirror. "Your parents."

I turn, and see that our car is right behind us. Dad must have hightailed it down from the parking lot to have caught up with us so soon. He grins and waves, and Em and I wave back, and my mom closes her mouth and stops saying whatever she's been saying. She wanted to come with us, in this car, so Dad could get back to the office, but he decided it was too late. He'd rather go home and have a drink, he said.

I turn back, look out the front window. I don't like looking at them together.

"Is everything all right?" Em asks, looking over at me as the light turns green and she starts the car forward.

"What do you mean?"

"With you. School. Friends. How are you doing, Sarah?"

"Great!" I say. "I got honours last report card, and I've got lots of friends."

"I'm sure you do," she says, and smiles, but her eyes stay on my face until the light changes back to green.

I did have a lot of friends, but mainly the only one I ever see these days is Heather. It's Heather who originally figured it out, based on her own experience. She even told her mom, and her mom says I can come over and stay with them if things get nasty. I'll still be able to go to school if I do that – maybe it will even look to other people like everything is normal, which it wouldn't if I was staying with one of my brothers. Not to mention the hour on the bus I'd have to take. I wish she hadn't told her mom.

When I asked her what she meant by "nasty," Heather said, "Tense. Shouting all the time. One time my mom even hit my dad across the face."

I close my eyes, press my teeth together, then open my eyes and tell Em how much I love her outfit, and right away we're onto the subject of shopping, which we both love. We talk about how we might go over to the mall tonight or tomorrow morning, and I tell her I've already asked my friend Heather if she wants to come along, and then I say I'm sorry that I've done that. Em says that it's fine, she's welcome. She doesn't know that I wasn't apologizing.

Cousin Em always says how broke she is, warning me to become anything besides an artist, but she always buys me something delicious. Something that I have to hide when I get home. She bought me my first lipstick. Wash-off tattoos when I was eleven. Red silk boxer shorts last time.

"Heather's dad's on his third marriage. Her mom's okay – I hang out there all the time. Heather's okay, too."

Em looks over at me again. Then she looks back at the road.

"You're sure everything's all right?"

"I'm sure," I say, and nod.

5.

I can't use Velma, my usual travel agent. Velma is this matronly-type woman who has arranged my (albeit infrequent) trips for years, and is one of the most fervent and vocal supporters of my art. Not that she knows anything about art, but she's sincere, and she's convincing, and I've sold a few paintings thanks to her. Without saying anything, Velma would make me feel guilty for wasting the last of my money on this trip when I have no guarantees of any future income ever, and in order to reduce my guilt I would be forced to explain to her that I have to go to Vancouver because I can't get any work done until I do. And then I would have to tell her why. So I get the name of another agent from Arnold, the guy who serves me coffee at the Internet café down the street from my studio.

Because of the condition of my VISA card, it is necessary for me to go over to the new agent's office in person to pay for my tickets with a certified cheque. The route to his office from my bank leads me within a block of the Canadian As Maple Pancake House in North York, and that starts me thinking about Sarah, thinking that maybe I should get her out of Vancouver for a while. For the spring holidays at least, or something. Have her come east for Easter. "When Esther Went East for Easter": it was the title of a poem in a silly children's book I used to read to her. Sarah likes wordplay, too.

About four years ago, Uncle Geoff and Alicia Mae came to Toronto, bringing Sarah but leaving Tom and Fred back in Vancouver. It was the first time they had left the boys on their own at home. Tom was nearly twenty at that point, Frederick eighteen, so it wasn't that big a deal as far as I could see, although Alicia Mae still called at least once and sometimes twice a day to make sure they were all right. Called collect, which was expensive then. Not that it probably mattered all that much: Geoff has got them quite well off.

They'd been down in London visiting Aunt Isabel – it was about a year before she died – and afterwards they came up to Toronto for a weekend before flying back to the west coast. Late on the Saturday morning, I met them at the Canadian As Maple Pancake House, which is not far from the Ontario Science Centre where we planned to spend the afternoon. It was almost April and the sun was out, but the day was unseasonably cool and all of us – but especially Alicia Mae – were well wrapped in hats and scarves and sweaters.

I was in a no-pay parking spot, which they were not, so we decided we would all go to the science centre in their car and leave mine where it was. After we'd finished eating, I popped back to my car to pick up an admission pass a friend had given me, while Geoff brought his car around.

I'd been holding the pass in my hand when I left home, but it wasn't in my handbag, and now it wasn't on the dashboard or on the front seats of the car. Finally I climbed right into my little Honda and started feeling around with my hands – under, beside, behind the seats. Straightening, I glanced up at the rearview mirror and saw that Geoff had pulled his rented car, a black Lincoln or something, into the empty parking stall behind me.

The three of them were just sitting there, not talking, waiting for me. Uncle Geoff was at the wheel and his well-wrapped wife was in the passenger seat. Behind them and between them was their Sarah, aged eleven at that time, and she looked so exactly the way I'd remembered looking at her age that the illusion drew a cold finger down my spine. It was her thinness, her straight pale brown hair, her large dark brown eyes taking it all in. I watched her reflection for several moments in my rearview mirror, feeling as though I were looking into my own past.

The first time my mother was in hospital, she was there for

quite a while, and Uncle Geoff came East and stayed for nearly a week. Several times he and Aunt Isabel drove me over in Aunt Isabel's big black car to see my mother, and I would sit quietly in the back seat, not wanting to be with them. It made my insides hurt to even think of going to the hospital.

When we got there, Uncle Geoff and I would get out and stand on the sidewalk, him leaning back against the car and packing tobacco in his pipe, me standing still beside him, while Aunt Isabel disappeared through the heavy-looking metal-and-glass front doors on her way up to my mother's room. Perhaps she had to help my mother out of bed and help her get her robe on, because it was always quite a long time before the two women appeared at the window. Then my mother would wave at me and at Uncle Geoff down on the pavement. She would blow us kisses. And we would wave back at my mother.

After that, Uncle Geoff and I would go for an ice-cream cone and wait until Aunt Isabel was finished visiting.

I'm sure they thought they were being kind to take me there, but the shame nearly overwhelmed me as I waved to my mother from the street. Part of it was fear of being seen by someone I knew from school. Part of it was fear that I might start to cry in public. But most of it was a fear that I didn't understand till later, of something too soft to grip, something dark and permanent.

I remembered that feeling exactly when I saw Sarah sitting in the back seat of that rented Lincoln with her parents. It was an eerie déjà vu and now it's back again. And it returns once more as I put the airline tickets on the table near the door of my studio, which is exactly where I found the admission pass to the Ontario Science Centre after Uncle Geoff had paid for all four of us to get in.

6.

Heather is heading across the street toward our place before we've even stopped in the driveway. She's wearing her new denim flares and the little blue short-sleeved T-shirt that shows her navel when she moves, and her blond hair's pulled way up on her head so it falls in all directions like the laser lamp in Mom's sewing room. As Em is getting out of the car, I watch Heather bouncing and grinning across the lawn towards us, braces on her teeth, and I get this feeling like, Oh my God I've never really looked at her before. And I know that she will never in a million years see what I see in my cousin's outfit, let alone my cousin.

The two of us carry Em's suitcase up to the guest room and put it down, and a minute later Em comes up and takes off her hat and the jacket of her suit. Under it she's wearing this slinky black satin-looking camisole, or maybe it's a slip. She says how much she envies us living where spring comes when it's still winter everywhere else, and then she goes into the bathroom to freshen up. She is so compact. She moves with such self-confidence. I want to be just like her.

"Don't you say a single word about my parents," I hiss at Heather the instant we're alone.

"I won't," Heather says, sitting down on the edge of the bed beside the suitcase and stretching out her legs. "Why do you think I would?"

I turn away from her, pull the curtains open and look down into the garden.

"She's great," she says.

"What do you know?" I say, not turning. "You only met her two minutes ago."

"I love her hair."

"Hair's got nothing to do with it. You'd have to see her paintings. And her studio." Which you never will, I think.

"What's eating you all of a sudden?"

"Nothing."

When Em comes back she opens her suitcase, to take the pressure off the stuff inside, she says, smiling at us. She gets out a bright orange silk blouse which she puts on, buttons, and tucks into her skirt. After that, all three of us go downstairs so Em can have a drink with my mom and dad, and Heather and I can have a pop.

It always feels to me like Em is closer in age to me than to my parents, but she isn't. She just acts like it.

When we come into the living room, my father looks at Heather's navel and so does my mother. My dad's looking curious, like he's never seen a girl's navel before, and my mom is looking totally burned up. I am mad at the different way the two of them react.

"Sarah, get the hors d'oeuvres from the fridge," Mom says in that bitchy little voice she only has the nerve to use at home. "And a shirt for Heather to put on."

"Oh, Alicia," Em says. "Heather's right in style."

"I don't care what she is," my mother says, smoothing her skirt carefully before she sits down on it. "She's a guest in our home."

You don't tell guests what to wear is what I'm thinking, but Heather's already half way up to my bedroom to get the shirt for herself. She was just checking to see what she could get away with, or showing off for Em. She's been over here before.

Heather's mom and dad have been divorced since she was ten. Her mom stays at home all day, living off the alimony. Her dad must be pretty well off, because he doesn't seem to work much either, and he's got two whole families to support in addition to himself. He and his third wife are always playing golf.

Heather gets almost anything she wants, and she's allowed to wear whatever she wants. She says it'll be a lot easier for me that way, too, but I don't think it will. I can't see that there will be any advantages at all.

Some of the things that Heather recognizes from before her own parents got divorced are these:

- my dad's always out of town on meetings;
- my dad's almost never home for dinner;
- my dad's usually in a good mood with everyone but my mother;
- my dad goes to the gym all the time;
- my dad will sometimes hang up the phone in the middle of a conversation if I walk in on him;
- my dad hardly ever gets mad at me any more;
- my mother looks either like she's scared or mad or going to start crying any minute, all the time.

I am never getting married.

7.

I stare at my in-basket, my mind set on a backward twist and tumble by the name and address in the Sender column.

scott.turnbull@gardanz.ca

I should go back and do some more work before I open this message.

I should finish the entire painting, if it takes weeks or even months, before I open this message.

If I click on this message, the nude on the chair will never be the same.

The nude on the chair will never be the same even if I don't click on this message.

I click.

Dear Em, he writes.

Yesterday afternoon I was down at the VAG. First time in a decade, to be truthful. There was an acrylic abstract there called Toronto's City Hall, *and I noticed the name of the artist, and I thought, "That couldn't be her, could it?"*

In the warmth of the Internet café, I look down at my left hand and remember the feel of the roll of white tape around the heavy school ring that made it small enough to fit my finger, how dirty the tape used to get. I recall the afternoon when I dropped it into his open hand, the surprise on his face. How I turned away before the surprise changed to hurt or anger.

I feel my throat close, swallow. Arnold offers me another coffee, but I shake my head. I shut the connection down.

Back in my studio, I feel a painful and familiar tenderness as I move the brush down the forearm of the nude upon the chair. I feel as though I am stroking the model's arm, instead of trying to give shape and substance to its representation.

As I feared, the work begins to change, and I put the brushes and paints away before I ruin it.

8.

It took Em more than an hour to get dressed after brunch, which she barely touched even though there were waffles which she loves – I once watched her eat three of them at some place in Toronto she took us to called the Maple Pancake House or something – and now, after we're already in the car, she's gone back inside to change again.

"You look awesome," I tell her when she returns. This time she's wearing a pair of black trousers, a dark purple sweater with little metallic threads in it that brings out the highlights in her hair, and a grey suede jacket even though it looks like rain.

"Thanks," she breathes, looking over at me. She does look awesome, but she also looks scared.

She turns the key. The engine is already running, and there's a terrible grinding noise that makes us wince. She turns the car off.

"Excuse me," she says, opening her door. "I'll be right back."

And she is gone up the walk into the house again.

I am disappointed at her nervousness, at the way it's using up her attention. She still hasn't told us who she's meeting, but she said she might not be back for dinner even. This could be our only time alone.

"Good God," she says when she finally slams herself back again into the car. "I'm sorry. My stomach's a little upset. I'm going to make you late."

"I don't care," I tell her. "I hate piano lessons." I sigh and slide the book back up on my lap. "They're horrible. I bet you never had to take them."

She starts the car again. "I wouldn't have minded," she says. "I always wished I had."

I start telling her awful it is to practice, how Miss Maynard always makes me feel like a ten-year old at the concert she puts on every year, but Em's paying no attention. She even makes a wrong turn on the way to Miss Maynard's house – going left when I've just finished telling her to go right.

When she finally gets into Putnam Street, I decide it's now or never and I tell her.

She glances at me, startled. "What?"

"My mom and dad will be getting a divorce," I say again. I am looking ahead, at the road, not at her.

"What makes you think that?" she says, in a tiptoe kind of voice.

"Heather." I sigh and look over at her. "She's been through it once or twice – "

She's slowing down the car, and it looks like she's struggling to get her mind to where we are. "What do you mean 'once or twice'?"

"Her dad's on his third marriage." I told her that already. On the way home from the airport. I thought she was paying attention then. A big sigh comes out of me. "She's been getting me prepared."

"She might just be imagining.... She might just want you and her to – "

I look out the passenger window. "Also, my dad said something about it to my brothers. I'm not supposed to tell anyone that they told me."

She goes silent at that.

"I wish they'd get it over," I say. I need to speak in a low tone or else my voice might crack. "I don't want to watch." I sit up straighter, which feels a little better. "I'm going over to Heather's when it happens – her mom says it's okay. Or maybe stay with Thomas and Jaylene."

Now she's pulling the car off to the side of the road, and she stops on the shoulder beside an empty lot. She looks straight ahead and not at me. Which I'm grateful for. But then if she was the kind of person to stare at me, look like she felt sorry for me, try to pry stuff out of me, I wouldn't be talking to her this way.

"I'm not going to be a bit like my mom when I grow up," I say. "I'm going to be like you."

She usually smiles when I say this, but she doesn't this time. She says, "Maybe it'll all blow over. Sometimes these things do."

I shake my head. "Don't tell anyone I told you."

"I won't," she says. "I won't."

It hasn't made me feel any better to have told her; in fact, I think I might feel worse.

Damn my parents anyway. Damn my mom and dad.

"Sarah," she says, now turning to look at me.

"What?"

"Tell me about your mother."

"What about my mother?"

"Do you think everyone knows but her?"

I move my feet against each other, clap my shoes together once or twice.

"I think she knows," I say.

Cousin Em nods, then looks into the rearview mirror like she's waiting for someone to appear behind us.

"I don't even like Heather," I confide at last. "I don't even like hanging out with her. We have nothing in common except this."

"I know what you mean," she says.

9.

Swallowing hard, I turn away from him and begin to walk as fast as I can toward the front doors of the school. The halls are full of students slamming locker doors, calling to one another – sweet sounds, familiar voices I will never hear again.

I swallow, swallow, walking fast down the middle of the hall, pretending not to hear when someone calls my name. Finally I gain the big front doors, push them open, get out into the coolness of the afternoon – only to have the afternoon turn on me, too, grip at my heart as well. It's Friday. It's September. The whole weekend lies ahead.

At the foot of the sidewalk at the front of the school is the big black car, my aunt at the wheel, waiting, relieved to see me at last. I've already put the boxes of everything that was in my locker into her trunk, and we've met with the principal and got the papers I will need to take with me. As we left his office, Mr. Belanger remarked in a quiet voice that I heard perfectly on my control. Aunt Isabel agreed I was coping with remarkable strength with everything.

"Better than I am, often," she said, voice catching.

Her doctor has decreed that "after everything with Edith" she's not strong enough to cope with the raising of a teenager. Uncle Geoff found a boarding school on the west coast, in Victoria – close enough for him to come and see me when he can. My aunt's neighbour, Mrs. MacNeill, says he's been very generous and thoughtful for a man, especially one who's single. She doesn't know he has a girlfriend, but he does. He told me about her at the funeral. Her name's Alicia Mae, and he's certain I will like her.

Our house, mine and my mother's, has been dismantled, everything Aunt Isabel thinks I might want someday put into storage, the rest auctioned off or given to Goodwill. In two hours I'll be on the plane.

I am almost at the car when I see the smile in Aunt Isabel's eyes turn to surprise and feel a hand on my shoulder.

I turn.

Scott holds out his hand, opens it, and his ring is on it. The roll of grey adhesive tape looks heavier than the ring itself.

"What's this about?" he says, red-faced.

I blink, and feel my throat go tight.

"Tell me, Em." He shoves his open hand toward me. "Tell me. What is this?"

Brown eyes, hurt. Freckles that I will never see again.

I gather breath, say on the exhalation, "I am moving."

His anger vanishes. "You're doing what? To where?"

"B.C. My uncle lives there."

"Now?"

I nod.

"But you can't," he says in disbelief. "We're going out. Tonight. You told me that you could."

In a tone low enough that my voice won't break, I say the last I expect I'll ever say to him. "So I lied," is what I say. And shrug. And add, "I'm sorry."

When I get into the car, my head turned away from him toward the street, Aunt Isabel reaches across to pat my shoulder.

"It's good to cry," she says. "Good for you. It's good to cry at last."

10.

Her meeting's in this restaurant called The Fisherman, right down at the waterfront. It is nearly two blocks from our parking space and it's after two o'clock, so we have to practically run to get there – Em looking at her watch every few seconds. We're both totally out of breath when we finally arrive.

Em takes the time to smooth her clothes, smooth her hair, smooth her breath a bit, and so do I, before she grips the big brass handle of the door and pulls.

Inside, the restaurant smells a little sweet, like flowers, and a little bit like garlic. Not at all like fish, thank God. It's dark near the entranceway where we are, bright near the windows opposite which go from floor to ceiling. The place is carpeted in red, furnished with blond-wood tables and chairs with sturdy-looking legs. There are a couple of white-haired couples drinking coffee at a table near the window, and at another table overlooking the water there's one guy by himself. Otherwise, the place is empty.

I can't see the face of the guy too well because the light's behind him, but his hair is totally grey. From the way Cousin Em's been talking, I was expecting someone younger, someone more her age. But there's no one else around, so that has to be the one. He's looking right at us but he isn't getting up.

Em, beside me, raises her hand, and now he does stand up. You can see he's still uncertain but he begins to walk towards us. As he gets closer and I can see him better, I realize he's not as old as I first thought. He's got short sandy-gray hair and a thin face, lean body. He's wearing off-white chinos, grey loafers, a dark-green flannel jacket. Glasses. Sort of good looking in the kind of way my mom likes – the Robert-Redford-meets-Eddie-Bauer look.

When he gets close enough that his presence moves the air, he says to Cousin Em, "It is you." He smiles. "You haven't changed a bit."

She's taken a step so she's behind me and I feel her hands go to my shoulders, rest there. She laughs, then says in the same kind of husky voice she was using in the car when she told me about the time she saw him last, "Neither have you. It's good to see you, Scott."

He looks at me and then again at her. Em presses her hands gently on the outsides of my shoulders, and says, "This is my cousin, Sarah." Like she's proud. Presses again, and says, "Sarah, Mr. Turnbull."

He holds out a hand and shakes my hand, looking right into my eyes. "I'm Scott," he says. "How do you do?" Then he looks back at Cousin Em. "She looks a lot like you."

I feel her suddenly relax.

"She's spending the afternoon with me," she says. "Bit of a family crisis."

You can see the disappointment cross his face before he pushes it away.

"Great," he says, actually sounding like he means it. He points to the table he's selected near the window. "We'll just get another chair." He goes away to find one.

"I don't need to stay," I tell her, turning. "I'm feeling a lot better."

"I know you are," she says.

"He's cute," I say. "You two should be alone." I feel suddenly stronger, knowing who she's meeting, knowing why the meeting's made her nervous. "I can meet you someplace later. I can even take the bus home on my own." I wink. "I won't tell a soul."

"In a little while," she says, "if you still want to go, you can." She nods at Mr. Turnbull, who is waiting at the table to draw out a chair for her.

"There's time for that," she says and smiles. "There's time for everything. Come have a cup of coffee with us first."

I start to protest again, but she puts her fingers up against her lips and shakes her head.

"Do it for me," she says.

Cool

Without raising her sunglasses from her eyes or even looking up at him, Katerina said, "I'll see you next year, then."

He looked out at the hot sea, unwilling to nod or blink or acknowledge in any way that he'd heard what she had said.

Bathers had strewn themselves along the beachfront, their umbrellas and towels and bright plastic buckets and beach balls scattered as far as he could see. He felt alone with her in spite of that.

If he turned his head he would have to work at it to find the mouth of the inlet. It would be remarkable only by the slightly hazier greens and blues and browns that extended into sky beyond it. But he did not turn his head.

He did not look at her, either. He kept his attention on the sea sails and on not moving his bare feet – his soles felt scorched from coming this far across the sand – but he was aware of all of her. She too was still, on her low beach chair, the brown smooth skin of her belly forming one darker crease along her waist. At the edge of his vision were long tanned arms and legs, long fingers and long toes, nails bronzed and shining. She was wearing a modest suit, striped mustard gold and scarlet, the halter top so perfectly constructed, it seemed to him, to possess her small round breasts. The thought of them made his heart hurt.

"If I come back again next year, that is," she said. "I may decide to get a job instead."

And God, his heart was breaking now, and still she didn't move, not even one small gesture. She'd told him how she laid herself out for twenty minutes at a time so the sun would strike her in exactly the places she wanted it to, and that she'd even accounted for the movement of the earth against the sun.

After a long time he said flatly, "I said my parents were leaving. That doesn't mean I have to."

He'd imagined it as he came looking for her across the beach, how he would tell her about his parents' change of plans, and she would protest, urge him to find a way to stay. He'd been certain that, if nothing else, their knowledge of what was in the boat house must bind her to him.

Now she did begin to move, not in response to what he'd said but to a tiny beeping sound from the inside of her beach bag. She swung her legs to the side and gingerly lowered those slender brown feet onto the sand, gathering lotions from the shade of the chair into the bag.

"Where would you stay?" she asked him, her smooth brown hair falling forward, obscuring her face as she tucked and pulled the bag shut.

"With my aunt and uncle," he said. "I may decide to do that."

He'd picked up this manner of speaking from her – I may decide this, I may decide that – dipping into options as though anything were possible and the future didn't really matter anyway. In fact, he'd already made the decision – grabbing his mother's suggestion that he could stay with an eagerness he'd never show with Katerina. With her, slowness was demanded, or else all would be lost. He did not know how he knew this, but he did.

She left the chair for him to fold and carry, and he ran to catch up with her, doing so just as sand gave way to stones and sticks and underbrush.

"Shall we go back tonight?" he asked her, using the words he'd put together while he walked out to see her. "See if it's still there?"

"It's dead," she said, head down, hair swinging. "Where's it going to go?"

~

But she did agree to come and then he had to wait for the time that she had set, which seemed to take forever – at least until the hour was nearly on him, and his aunt and uncle were still not back. Then, time started racing.

They'd been eager enough to keep him here because he could baby-sit for them. He'd done it already a few times since he arrived, and it hadn't been too bad. It consisted mainly in making sure his cousins, four and six, didn't fall into the fish pool or eat the berries his aunt was sure were poisonous.

But now instead of the half hour of absence he'd come to expect of them, they'd been gone for more than an hour, and as the time of his meeting with Katerina got closer, his cousins grew more and more demanding. Hungry, they said they were, even though they'd all eaten hamburgers and ears of corn already, and he didn't know or care what they might be allowed to eat at this point. He had to distract them with books and himself with watching the new family next door move in, including a tall bored-looking guy who sort of looked his age, but older.

Finally his aunt and uncle did show up – her running in her yellow summer dress and sandals, frantic to make sure her children were still alive after all that time without her. He thought they must have been held up somewhere against their will but his uncle was sauntering along after her, puffing slowly on his pipe, so maybe not.

As he made his way through the summer village to the place where he would meet her, he was thinking of how it would have been if he and Kevin had been the ones to find the dead man. He'd wanted to bring Kevin with him, so it could quite easily have happened, but his parents had said No, there'd be too many in the cabin as it was. Several times, especially since last night, he'd almost called long distance to tell Kevin what was going on, but he hadn't. Because then he'd have to explain about Katerina.

He and Kevin would have had bicycles, and they'd have run scared from what they'd seen, but pretending not to be. They'd have pedaled as fast as they could – shouting maybes at one another – to his parents or to the small police detachment house, to tell everyone what they'd seen.

But she'd said, "Let's not tell anyone," as they came back through the woods last night. "Let's see how long it takes."

"For what?"

"For someone else to find him."

"Why?" he asked, near-disappointment slowing him. "He's dead."

"That's the point," she said. "Exactly."

"He should be buried or something," he said to her. "Someone would want to know."

It seemed to him she was thinking about that, but after several minutes she said, "He's been dead a long time now. He doesn't even smell. What difference will it make?"

"It might be against the law," he said, his voice tight because her hand touched his just then.

"Yes," she said. "It might."

~

"Do you want to see my breasts?"

He looked at nothing else but her in the blue-green dusk, forcing himself to keep his eyes away from the dark shape he'd first thought to be a pile of rags when they'd come in last night. The boat house was overgrown with water weeds and land weeds, its planks and tiles fallen apart, away, cracks in the ceiling lifting light reflected from the water to the crumbled wood above, around them.

He nodded, and she undid her shirt and, bending forward from the waist, her long arms out as if to dive, she said, "Come closer then."

He did, shifting carefully down the boards, his feet barely moving the water, and she curled her fingers and took the hem of her halter top and lifted it, freeing her breasts, and lifted it again from off her head, shaking loose her hair. She moved her hands behind her to lean and rest on them, and her breasts came up hard and tight. White light wavered across her skin, and he was glad the man was dead and could not see her, too.

"You want to touch them?" she asked, her voice deep in her throat the way it had been when she'd talked about the man the night before, talked about making it a secret.

He raised a hand and brushed it against his shorts to clean it before he reached out gingerly across himself, to her. Still leaning back against her hands she sighed, and he moved his hand more surely over the smoothness and the roundness of the white, and the hard brown nub of nipple.

"Kiss me," she said, but when he bent toward her lips – his heart pounding, his heart about to scream – she said, "not there," and held his head and gently moved it down until he felt the nub against his tongue.

And God, it was too much for him and he had to turn away and slip into the water. There was a skim of oil across the surface, though there hadn't been a boat in years.

When he finally looked at her again, she was smiling, swinging one foot in the water, her eyes looking far off in the corner where the dead man was.

"I have a boyfriend in the city," she said. "I may decide to marry him."

~

He tried in his head to find ways to tell all this to Kevin while at the same time showing Kevin that he was not to laugh – he'd known Kevin all his life, and he knew he would want to laugh – or poke him in the side, or use words like "cool" or "lucky." He could not imagine how. And then he tried to picture all next winter or all his life not ever being able to tell any of this to anyone, and he could not do that either. He felt fierce and adult when he thought he might know something Kevin never would, but he also felt afraid. It made him turn in his hot bed, wouldn't let him sleep.

~

His uncle went to town to buy some liquor and he helped his aunt chase children up and down the beach to stop them from running into the sea and drowning, which took some doing since there were four of them, two sets of twins. They'd made their mother crazy, his mother said.

He saw as he was running back and forth that the tall guy in the cabin next to theirs had found Katerina on the beach. He saw that the guy was older than Katerina even, and he saw her move in her beach chair when she talked to him and lift the sunglasses from her eyes and smile. And his heart thudded at the thought that she might be telling him about the dead man in the boat house.

That night, he didn't dare to ask, didn't want to know, so relieved was he to be the one. But she wouldn't sit on the boards and dangle her feet in the water. Instead she led him closer to the bundle of rags and flesh he dreaded in the deep dusk corner, and when they came up to it he forced himself to look down into the dead man's face and saw the skin over his closed eyes was paper scorched that would crumble and fall apart if it were touched, wrinkled skin falling into little piles of dust, unlidding orbs, revealing sight.

He stepped back, not letting himself reach for her hand the way he wanted to.

~

At supper the next day they asked him if he wanted to go into the city with his uncle the next morning, or stay the last two weeks. He thought of the twins and how long the days were, and of Kevin in the city in the evenings wheeling along dark, smooth river valley paths, with no one to listen to. He thought of Katerina and said that he would stay.

When they'd eaten the fish, minutely broken before his aunt even gave it to them to make sure the bones were out, his uncle gave him money and told him to take his cousins to the park and then for ice cream, and not to come back until the ice cream was all gone. His aunt seemed fearful, as if there might be bones in ice cream, but his uncle held her firmly by the elbow and told them to go along. So, trailing children, off he went.

They hadn't been in the park too long, him running back and forth from the slides to the swings to the roundabout, when Katerina appeared, all skin tonight in a dress the colour of cantaloupe, bare arms, bare shoulders and bare tanned neck.

"Looks like you're tied up," she said, not looking at the children.

"Not for long," he said, standing at the edge of the playground where he had come to meet her.

"So am I," she said.

"How can you be?" he asked with a quick glance behind him to make sure all four were still alive. One of them was standing silently watching him, thumb stuck in his mouth.

She raised her shoulders until the skin touched the soft ends of her hair and said, "Maybe I'll see you tomorrow."

He turned away. He'd been stupid to think it would happen every night, but the keenness of his disappointment made him take the children early to get the ice cream over with so he could be alone. He came out the screen door of the ice cream shop in perfect time to catch a glimpse of cantaloupe and the tall guy's head on the overgrown path that would take them to the boat house.

~

He stood and looked where they had gone, and then he took the children by their hands and hurried them through the village streets to the small police detachment house, where out front a fat man in uniform was trying to fix a lawnmower in the cool of the shade of the house.

"There's a body," he told the policeman, breathing hard. "In the old boat house, up the inlet."

"What?" asked the man red-faced, raising his head to look at all the children – one of them crying now because his cone was empty, his ice cream fallen out.

"In the boat house," he insisted, feeling sick at the thought of the tall guy and Katerina, and sounding sick as well. "Up March Inlet. You'll need a boat to get him out."

"If this is some kind of…."

"It's not," he said, and to prove it he told the fat policeman what his name was, who his aunt and uncle were. He said, "You have to hurry."

~

It didn't matter how slowly he went, he was still ahead of them, the one with the replacement cone the slowest so he could guard it with his mouth and hand. He came into the cabin clearing ahead of all four of them, and looked up at the window in time to see his aunt leaned back against the table, his uncle lifting up her shirt. And his heart grew tight, and his throat was tight, as he felt the sweet salt taste of Katerina's skin against his tongue.

"Stay here," he said, herding the twins into a place where they were concealed beneath the trees. "Don't go near the fish pool, and don't go into the house until Mel's ice cream is all done."

He left them there and sprinted back toward the village, turning part way there to see that Mel had wandered into the roadway after him. So he sprinted back and gathered up the child into his arms and ran again, not daring to wonder where the others were. The child said nothing, but held on tight to him and he ran through the village, past the detachment house where the fat man was yelling from the police jeep at two other men in trucks and pointing in the direction of the water, ran through the park and the playground, and then slowed when he reached the path so he wouldn't trip on the roots and undergrowth.

Deep in the woods, he stopped. He'd heard the crashing and now he saw the tall guy stumbling through the underbrush toward him. He stood back from the path to let him pass.

His panting sounded hard and painful, and his face was white, and his T-shirt was marbled wet all down the front. "Jesus," he shouted at them as he went by. "Stay back, you guys. Stay back. There's a fucking dead man back there. Jesus. There's a fucking dead guy back there." On the wave of air he made as he went past, he left the smell of puke.

He put the child gently down on the ground beside him while he regained his own breath. Then he saw Katerina come cool and calm – stepping through the deep sunlit evening greenery toward him. She stopped when she saw him, then took his eyes with hers and drew them to the place where the tall guy in his fear had torn apart the path through the branches, making it wide where it had not been wide before. She looked at him and shook her head – and he saw that her eyes were shining, and that she was smiling, and that the one she was smiling at was him.

He looked at the child, and he looked back at her, and he thought about the people in the boat he could hear now, far off in the water.

And God, how he longed for Kevin.

Previous Publication Credits

The stories in this book first appeared in the following publications. All stories copyright by Mary W. Walters.

"Last Respects": *Grain Magazine*, February 1981, Volume IX, Number 1

"The Perfect Parent": *Chatelaine*, August, 1982

"Afternoon Visit": *NeWest ReView*, 1982

"The Gift of Maggie": *CBC Alberta Anthology*, September, 1980

"The Milk Wagon": *Dandelion*, 1989; *Alberta ReBound* (NeWest Press, 1990)

"The Wife": *Herizons*, 1984; *CBC Alberta Anthology*, 1984

"Print Dresses": *The Malahat Review*, 1985; *Alberta Bound* (NeWest Press, 1986)

"Honey Cat": Broadcast as a radio drama on *Vanishing Point*, CBC Radio, 1990; Rewritten as short story for serialization in *Culture Shock*, 1991.

"Keeping House": Published in a slightly different form in *Wascana Review*, Vol. 26, Nos. 1 & 2, Spring/Fall, 1991

"The Sign": *Prism International*, Summer, 1992

"The Hilltop": *Grain*, 1992; *CBC Alberta Anthology*, 1994

"Travelling by Mexico": *Dandelion*, Vol. 19, No. 2, 1992

"Men, Boys, Girls, Women": *Boundless Alberta* (NeWest Press, 1993)

"Show Jumping": *Prairie Fire*, Vol. 18, No. 4 Winter 1997-98; Journey Prize finalist, 1999; *Journey Prize Anthology* (McClelland & Stewart), 1999

"Cool": Finalist in 1997 *CBC/Saturday Night* Literary Competition

Editor's Note

Mary W. Walters has an uncanny gift for laying bare the thoughts of characters who inhabit the liminal domain between magic realism and contemporary urban life. Written over the span of twenty years, the stories collected in *Cool* explore the subtleties of being human in a shifting world, and the challenges of being caught in unfamiliar territory without a map.

The work of Mary W. Walters was unfamiliar territory for me when I accepted the invitation of Candas Jane Dorsey, publisher of River Books, to be the outside editor of *Cool*. With delight I discovered the skillfully drawn portrait of the newly orphaned Emmie in "Last Respects", the riotous satire of "The Perfect Parent" and the suspense of "Afternoon Visit". In "The Gift of Maggie" I shared in the fantasy of striking it lucky, then I was brought to earth again in the horror of "The Milk Wagon". The rest of the unfolding stories drew me further into Walters' world, where even the most outlandish events felt unsettlingly familiar, and I found a new appreciation for the miracle that is everyday life.

The journey spirals through time toward "Relatives and Friends", written on request for this collection, visiting an Emmie grown-up since "Last Respects". The title story, "Cool", then invites the reader back to the world of young adulthood explored in several of the stories in the collection: unsettling, uncharted and profoundly satisfying.

Each of the sixteen stories is a beautifully crafted gem, as multifaceted and brilliant as their author.

—Timothy J. Anderson

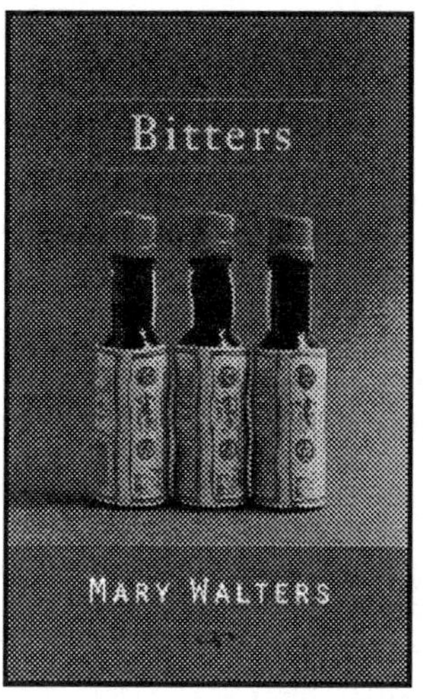

A woman torn by the life she is leading and the lie she is living.

When Maggie Townsend, wife of Archie Townsend, MLA, longs for a more interesting, artistic and bohemian life she is drawn into an illicit affair with the sexy writer and thinker Zeke Avery, a man she has not seen since university. Maggie soon has her hands full trying to manage a job, a family, and her affair with the tormented writer. Things become even more complicated on the eve of the provincial election when Maggie's worlds collide.

PRAISE FOR MARY WALTERS' NOVEL BITTERS:

"Readers are swept full force into the exhilarating hell of leading a double life... Walters keeps the pages turning in what feels more like the events in real lives lived..." —Bill Robertson, Star Phoenix

IF YOU LIKED THIS BOOK... YOU MAY ALSO ENJOY THESE TITLES FROM BOOKS COLLECTIVE IMPRINTS

Send All Orders To:
The Books Collective
214-21-10405 Jasper Ave.
Edmonton AB, T5J 3S2
(pay by cheque or money order, add 3$/book for shipping, Canadian orders add 7% GST, US orders pay in US funds,)
SUBSCRIBERS GET 30% OFF! WRITE AND FIND OUT HOW!

The Rain is Full of Ghosts By Zoe Landale
ISBN: 1-895836-81-6 • $16.95
River Books • November 2000 • Novel
In Zoe Landale's first novel, we are shown how one young woman's life, work and loves are affected by an overwhelming loss. What comfort can her Family Ghost bring Ingeborg? And how will that connect her with her family remaining in Denmark, and the new family she is building in Canada?

Violin / Vajolin By Marijan Megla
Edited and transposed into standard English by Reg Silvester
ISBN: 1-895836-60-3 • $15.95.
Slipstream/River Books • September1998 • Short Stories
Marijan Megla's uses his own unique form of phonetic English to give an incredible immediacy to his narrative, bringing alive a post-war Croatian village. The book's richly drawn characters and humorous intrigues breathe with the author's earthy first-person prose and sly wit as he captures the lives of common folk. Reg Silvester's "transposed" versions of the stories provide the flavour of the originals while serving as a key to crack the phonetic code.

Gypsy Messenger By Marijan Megla
ISBN: 1-895836-82-4 • $13.95
River Books • September 2000 • Poetry
This is a lyrical invocation of the Romany way of life by irrepressible story teller Marijan Megla. Here in Gypsy Messenger, we are treated once again to the Eastern European people and scenes that Megla makes his very own. From travellers to villagers, Megla's characters speak for us in the real voices and images of their daily lives.

Fruitbodies By Mary Woodbury
ISBN: 1-895836-17-4 • $15.95
River Books • 1996 • Poetry
Here is a powerful collection about the many faces and ages of woman: the loving woman, the creative woman and the ageing woman. The work celebrates all of life with laughter, tears and silence. Honouring the body, mind and spirit of what it means to be a passionate human being, these poetic reflections allow readers to experience their own vulnerability and joy.

The Edmonton Queen (not a riverboat story): inside a dynasty of drag By Darrin Hagen
ISBN: 1-895836-46-8 • $15.95
Slipstream/River Books • 1997 • Autobiography
As Edmonton's best-known drag queen, Hagen's meteoric career has crossed over into mainstream theatre, music and media. Hagen's book chronicles a time when he found a family within Edmonton's drag queen world, a world filled with acceptance and love, power struggles for adoration and attention, and losing battles with AIDS.—Wendy Boulding

Llamas in the Snow By Cullene Bryant
ISBN: 1-895836-04-2 • $12.95
River Books • 1993 • Short Stories
A readable, sensitive collection of short fiction about the verities of human existence. Her scenarios are moving, intense and occasionally chilling as she peels away the facade of the everyday to reveal the complexities beneath.

Hector's War By George Wing
ISBN: 1-895836-68-9 • $15.95
River Books • November 1999 • Novel
Hector Plouvier joins the army and goes to fight in the trenches in France. When the dust and smoke clear from the battlefield, Hector leaves his identity tags with the corpse of a fallen comrade. From that moment on he is dead to his past. Hector's War is a story of degradation and redemption, of loss and salvation, and of devastation and renewal in the lives of Hector and all of the people he touches.